ZANZIBAR KWA HERI

(Farewell, Zanzibar)

Patricia K. Polewski

 www.trafford.com

North America & international
toll-free: 1 888 232 4444 (USA & Canada)
fax: 812 355 4082

The front cover is of:

Beached dhows in Dar Es Salaam harbor. Dhows are washed ashore by incoming tide and secured by ropes to any palm tree. Receding tide leaves dhows beached and exposed for needed maintenance.

Back cover

Sunset over the headwaters of the Nile at Jinja, Uganda.

CONTENTS

PROLOGUE

In 1964 the African natives overthrew the Sultan of Zanzibar and the Arab government that was governing the island.

This inexperienced new regime passed some strange laws. One of which was that young women could not leave Zanzibar unless they paid 56,000 shillings to the government. For most, the sum was far too high.

The purpose of the law, though denied, was to keep young Asian girls on the island as first, second or third wives of the ruling establishment.

This novel is about one girl's escape from Zanzibar and the terrific problems she had before finally finding her safe harbor.

The author was living in Tanzania and heard heart rending stories, especially from young men who were trying so desperately to get their sweethearts and sisters off Zanzibar. Real names have not been used. Real events have.

Sunday evening gathering of mostly Indian people on the Azania Front Park facing the Dar Es Salaam harbor. An opportunity to see and be seen. (Circa 1969)

CHAPTER ONE

Melissa didn't notice the tall Arab carrying a rolled-up carpet until she bumped into him. She asked, "Saidi, can it really be you?"

"Melissa!" He set the carpet down on its tightly rolled end. "I didn't know you were still on Zanzibar! So many people have gone, most of your friends too, I think it is so?"

Crowds of people pressed around them on all sides, Arabs, native Swahili Zanzibaris and a scattering of Asians, everyone intent on his own business.

"Yes," she agreed sadly, "Some are in Canada, many in Tanzania. You know that my parents are dead?"

"I have been told. *Pole sana*, Melissa." His face showed real concern for her.

"I heard that you work in the office of a dentist. Do you still work there?"

"No longer. Dr. Rodrigues left six months ago for UK And I haven't been able to find work since. I live with my cousins."

"The government took over your family's coconut plantations?"

"Yes. Of course. The trees are not cared for, not even harvested. Even if they gave them back now, they are almost worthless." She shrugged her shoulders.

"Why do you not leave Zanzibar? There is no future here for Asians—or Arabs for either, as I know well."

"I can't leave." She spoke softly pretending to look at the carpet so he wouldn't see the tears in her eyes.

"The 56,000 shillings?"

"Yes—56,000 shillings. The Government might as well say I must pay a million pounds for a permit to leave. I am not allowed to work here, and our property was confiscated after the 1964 Revolution, so where would so much money come from? That is the total wages of a professional man for seven full years!" Melissa sounded angry and very frightened.

"No government should be able to tell unmarried women they must pay ransom to leave or stay and be forced to marry Swahili men much older than they are, not of their religion and already married to other women." Saidi said reasonably.

"Yes." said Melissa "There are fewer professional and business people here every day. The Africans do not trust the Asians or the Arabs, and Arabs and Asians don't trust Africans. There are no longer any English left to think about in any way at all. Instead we have many Chinese and I don't think many people trust them either." She sighed deeply.

The constant flow of traffic around them provided a kind of privacy of its own. No one could possibly catch more than a word or two. Some of the traffic was on foot and some on bicycle. Asian women in saris and black women in the all-enveloping garment called *buibui*, which means spider. As they hurried down the streets they sometimes looked like many giant spiders. They mingled with Sikhs with full beards and perfectly wrapped turbans. They were always neatly dressed, and wearing their trademark steel bangle bracelet. They contrasted with the Arabs wearing lengths of plaid cloth wrapped snugly around the waist and extending below the knees. Older black Muslim men strolled by wearing long white robes.

"I remember that it was arranged between your family and the Da Silva's that you and their son, Antonio, would marry. Is he still here?"

"No, Tonio is in Tanzania. He's an accountant there with the Government and he's saving money, but 56,000 is such an impossible sum."

"If I had it, I would give it to you. Allah would repay me! It was your father who lent me the money to buy my dhow. I repaid him as soon as I could, but I owe your family a favor."

"Ah, Saidi, someone else would have helped a good captain like you even if my father had not. It is so good to have a chance to talk to you again."

"Consider, Melissa," Saidi said hesitatingly, "there is a way other than finding so much money. You know I am an honest man. I buy good carpets on the Persian gulf and I sell them for all I can get for them. But I have as little to do with governments and their regulations as possible. I know that some of my carpets come from Russia, some from Iraq, some from Iran. I call them Persian carpets. The merchants I sell them to know by the pattern and weave exactly where everything comes from. Some of my goods were smuggled into trade. I ask few questions. That way I am told few lies."

Then he laughed and looked at Melissa searchingly

while he said, "If you were an illegal carpet, I could get you out of here easily. Can you swim?"

"Yes, but not very well, nor for very long. Why?"

"I don't think you would have to swim far. If you want me to try, I think I can get you to Dar es Salaam."

"Saidi, I do want you to try, I want it more than anything, but I can't bear to think of what will happen to us if your plan fails. Jail for you, at the very least. The Government would force me into marriage with some old man who already has three wives." She sighed and looked hopeless.

"Inshallah." (It is as Allah wills) said the Arab with a shrug of his wide shoulders.

"If you are willing to risk it, then tell me what I should do." Melissa said eagerly.

Saidi thought a moment as he rubbed a big work-worn hand over his fierce looking mustache and the black stubble on his chin.

Finally he said, "Go home. Tell the people you live with that you might be taking a journey soon. They are not to worry and not to report you missing for several days, if at all. Don't say goodbye to anyone. Sew a small purse to the inside of a bathing costume, wear your dress over it and don't take anything else. Come down to Dhow Harbor tomorrow morning about five. If you wear a lace scarf on your head, anyone on the street at that time will think you are on your way to an early mass."

"I don't have much to put in the purse." She said apologetically.

"That doesn't matter. When we get to Dar es Salaam, Antonio will be there to care for you. But you will need money for a telephone call and you can't carry it in your hand and swim. I will see you in the morning at Dhow Harbor." Re-shouldering his rolled up carpet, he said, "*Salamu.*" and disappeared into the swirling crowd.

Now her step was quicker, excitement made it hard not to break into a run and yet she couldn't help but feel a bit frightened, too. By this time tomorrow she would be in Dar es Salaam, or at the bottom of the Indian Ocean, or perhaps in Zanzibari detention.

The Island had been home to her all her life. Her parents were born there, too, but they were dead and all their property confiscated. Her father was killed during the Revolution and her mother died soon afterward. The death certificate said she died of malaria, but Melissa thought that a broken heart would have been a better diagnosis. Malaria was only the final nail in her coffin.

She knew that escape was what her parents would want for her. They certainly would not want her to stay on Zanzibar as a charity case and there was little hope that she would find work. Her light olive skin, her fine, small features and soft, long black hair would always mark her as different, as non-African. Not having work was hard. The danger of forced marriage was worse.

Her grandparents had come from Goa, a tiny part of India long controlled by the Portuguese. But Melissa was not Portuguese, although her Portuguese name and her Catholic religion came from them.

She certainly didn't feel Indian either. She shrugged her shoulders thinking it was not her fault that she couldn't live in Zanzibar, where she had been born seventeen years ago. She'd reached the gate of her cousin's home and called out, "Rita, I'm home!"

"In here Melissa. We are having tea. Did you have any luck today?"

"I think I may have had some good fortune. Don't ask any questions because I can't give you any answers, but perhaps things may be better now."

She accepted the cup of tea her cousin poured out for her, and sat down at the table with Rita and Roberto. She'd slathered mango preserves on a piece of bread and ate it with the best appetite she'd had in months.

It was difficult to hide her excitement during the evening. Several times she looked at her watch to see if it had stopped.

"Time for bed," she said finally, and added, "Thank you both for being so good to me. I will always be grateful and never forget you."

"Forget us!" Rita exclaimed.

"What do you mean?" Roberto asked.

"Nothing, except that whatever might happen to any of us, I am forever grateful to the kind people who took in their eleven year old cousin and cared for her for six years."

A flicker of understanding passed between Rita and Roberto. They would not say it, but they knew that escape could never be far from Melissa's hopes and thoughts.

"Good night. Be sure to use your mosquito net." Roberto commanded.

"I will," she knew she needn't give them a story so they wouldn't report her missing. They understood her problem very well. She set the alarm for four a.m. But turned it off when an alarm in her brain woke her sooner. She sewed a small cloth change purse into the inside of her bathing suit, put some coins into it, and put it on with a simple cotton dress over it.

Finally the clock showed fifteen minutes to five, and Melissa quietly closed the door of her bedroom so that her absence wouldn't be noticed for a few hours. She carried her sandals and tiptoed down the stairs. The front door was locked and bolted and a bar was drawn across. It used to be uncommon to lock doors, but now people hardly felt safe with triple locks. She let herself out as quietly as she could and walked a few hundred feet before she turned and gave the house one last look. Then she hurried off towards Dhow Harbor.

Few people were out so early because it was still dark. The velvet black of the sky would turn to pale grey and then to an intense blue, all within the space of half an hour, much like a shade being slowly raised.

Dhow Harbor itself seemed to be getting ready for the morning tide, the last bits of work were being completed on dhows which lay on their sides as sailors greased the hulls. It was easy to spot Saidi who was pacing up and down on a small patch of shore near his vessel. It looked ready and waiting, and the sailors were aboard. Saidi spotted Melissa immediately and hurried toward her. "Have you had breakfast?"

"No, I was afraid to wake the household."

"Sit down and I'll get you a cup of coffee and a banana." A handful of men were sitting cross-legged on the sand talking quietly. Two boys were selling coffee from three feet high copper pots with little charcoal burners beneath them. In one hand, each boy carried two tiny porcelain cups that he clicked together enticingly as he walked along – an advertisement for coffee on the way. Most of the men bought coffee and sipped it slowly, while waiting for the tides to change.

Saidi handed her a banana, bought her a cup of coffee and said, "The dhow is ready and so is our crew. Finish your coffee, leave the cup with the men on the beach and come with me." She followed him aboard the old, but impressive looking sailing vessel. There were piles of oriental rugs on deck as well as below it. Melissa walked over to the carpets and asked, "Shall I wrap myself in one of these or crawl under a small pile of them?"

He laughed aloud and his big teeth flashed white in his weathered face as he said, "No. Just sit down over there and I'll return soon." He motioned her to the small canvas covered area toward the prow. "Don't worry, I think everything is going to be easier than you think." With that bit of encouragement for her, he strode off while calling orders to the sailors who were anxious to be underway.

Melissa sat quietly and thought about others who

had left Zanzibar by dhow. The thousands of slaves, the Asian girls now—so many people, with so many problems.

Everything on Saidi's vessel was handmade, and looked it. Food could be cooked on deck over a fire set on a little pile of sand. Water was stored in big drums. The latrine was a chair with slats and was attached to the side of the vessel. When the wind failed, the men passed the time by catching and salting fish; so there was fishing gear here and there. Luckily, the Indian Ocean and the Persian Gulf are warm waters because the only shelter for the sailors was a small canvas awning.

Melissa sat perfectly still under that shelter and watched the sailors cast off. In what seemed no time at all, the sails were up and filling out with the breeze and they were headed for the mainland of Africa, for Dar es Salaam.

She wanted to weep with fear and plain discouragement. Just when she believed the danger was over, it was right in front of them. The customs' officer greeted Saidi in a friendly way and went to work examining the cargo and looking at records. When his glance fell on Melissa he said pleasantly, "What kind of carpet is this? It looks to me like a Goan carpet!" He laughed aloud at his own little joke, but Melissa didn't find it amusing. His laugh might mean embarrassment, surprise, or even glee at catching a law breaker.

"Ndiyo, Bwana." Saidi agreed, "It is indeed a Goan carpet, but to me all carpets are Persian, you know that by now!"

"Ah yes, I do know that."

"While you are here, please take a cup of coffee with me, will you not?" Saidi asked politely.

A large copper Arabian pot on a charcoal filled stand was at arm's reach. The African said he would enjoy a cup while he checked over some of the records. Melissa looked mutely at Saidi, who said nothing to her, but acted as though the two men were alone. They sipped coffee while the official finished his work.

"Well, all is in order, my friend. I must go now. While this wind blows, there is no rest for the customs' officer." He extended his hand in farewell to Saidi who placed in it a red one hundred shilling note. Without so much as a glance at the bill, the African put it in his own pocket and said, "Asante na kwa heri, Salamu, Bwana." He was thanking Saidi and wishing him well.

"Asante, Bwana kwa heri." Saidi replied with a wave and a smile. The sailors went to the side to watch the customs' boat as it faded from view. One of them looked toward Melissa and made a sound of relief that resembled air being let out of a tire.

"Will he tell that I am here?" she asked Saidi anxiously.

"Oh no. He is my friend. I have known him for years but even so, if he thought you were here against your will, he would have taken you off. If the goods I have could not be accounted for, he would have taken them off, too."

"He took money to pay for his silence!" Melissa objected.

"He took money, yes. We understand each other. If he hadn't taken my money, I would worry would I not? He knows that."

"I think I understand." Melissa said, "Yet he works for the government and..." her voice trailed off because she didn't quite know how to finish her thought.

Saidi finished her sentence. "Men like him don't pass laws making it impossible for people to work in their own countries and impossible to leave if they don't have 56,000 shillings. *That* really is a bribe."

"Lie down, Melissa, and sleep before the sun gets too high in the sky."

She gratefully lay down on the expensive, silky carpets and was soon asleep. The heat of the sun on her back awoke her about nine. She stayed out of the way until Saidi said, "That is Dar es Salaam you see over there. Soon we will sail close to Silver Sands beach, about fourteen miles from the city. There will be people in the water and others on the shore or in the restaurant. One person more or less will not be noticed. We will help you slip over the side of the dhow that faces the sea. Then you must swim. The water becomes shallow soon and we can't go in any farther. After you are ashore, go and telephone Antonio." That seemed simple enough, but Saidi didn't seem quite satisfied—finally he added, "What will you do if you can't reach him?"

"I will just wait and try again and again." Melissa answered bravely, but she was worried. She'd be alone, almost penniless, no shoes and dressed in a wet swimming suit.

"Since it is Saturday, it is likely that he will be home sometime during the day, but if he isn't, I will be at the Rex Hotel this evening by seven. If you cannot reach Antonio where he lives, call me and I will find a way to come out and get you into town, and safe somewhere."

Melissa put her hand on his strong sun-darkened arm and said, "I can never thank you enough for doing this for me, Saidi."

He waved her thanks aside and replied, "If you are ever looking for me again, you know where to find me, Dhow Harbor in Aden, or in Zanzibar, Mombasa or Dar. Come now, off with the dress and over the side!"

She left her dress and sandals on the deck and Saidi and a sailor helped her over the side. She realized how far she would have to drop, and held tightly to their hands then forced herself to let go and she fell into the pleasantly cool ocean. She spat out salt water as she rose to the surface and realized gratefully that the water was calm.

She was swimming strongly but beginning to tire when she saw people not far from her playing in an inner tube. She put her feet down gingerly and found she could stand. The sand and even the sharp coral felt welcoming as she walked onto the shore. Her heart was beating fast—she was out of Zanzibar. She sat on the sand to recover her composure and realized she'd better go back into the water for her change purse. She walked into the ocean, and in the privacy of chest deep water, she gave a few sharp yanks at the threads holding the purse and it came away in her hand. Holding it dripping in her palm, she returned to the beach and lay there to dry off before entering the restaurant to phone Tonio.

She strolled in nonchalantly and sat at a little table. A waiter came, she ordered a Coca Cola and asked, "Telefoni?" He pointed her in the direction of the dance floor.

After drinking half her drink, Melissa left the table, went to the phone and started to look up Tonio's number. The semi-enclosed phone booth was full of sluggish flies and the phone book was barely hanging together as it dangled at the end of a frayed rope. Several pages had been torn out. She hoped fervently that his phone number would be there and that he would be home.

There was his name 'Da Silva, Antonio.' She put in her coins and dialed his number, almost forgetting to press the button which would enable her to hear him if he answered, even that thought made her nervous. The phone rang three times.

She was beginning to feel panic again, and then, "Da Silva here." came over the wires.

She sobbed as she said, "Tonio, I'm here!"

"You're here? Here in Dar?" he shouted. "How did you get here? No. Never mind. Where are you?"

"I am at Silver Sands resort. I'll be at a table near the road where the cars enter. Oh yes, would you please borrow a dress for me?"

"Yes, yes. I'll be right there. Don't move!" he ordered and hung up.

She returned to her table, picked up the unfinished drink and carried it to a table closer to the road. There was a large sign saying that the resort had showers and changing rooms for the benefit of guests. Melissa half smiled self-consciously as she thought she wouldn't be surprised if she were the first non-paying guest who had sneaked in by way of the sea.

Her reflection in the changing room mirror surprised her. She looked much as usual and even her hair was not particularly messy. She wore it loose and long and it curled slightly at the ends where it was still damp. The sun had given her cheeks a pinkish cast and she rarely used lipstick anyway.

"I wonder if he will still think I'm pretty?" she mused, but her reflection reassured her. She left the building and picked her way painfully across the hot, sharp coral gravel, sat down again with her now warm Cola to wait and watch the road.

"He told me when he bought a car that it belonged to a friend who emigrated to Canada, but I can't remember what color he said it was." She felt anxious as one car after another came down the dusty road.

"There!" she was sure now. "A cream colored VW." She got up from the table and nodded pleasantly at the employees ready to let down the chain barring the entrance. Even before Tonio could explain that he didn't want to come in, she had ducked under the chain and was getting into the car.

He smiled at her with such pleasure that he didn't need to say a word about how he felt. Expertly, he backed up to a wide place just off the road, turned the car around and started off for the city.

"Tell me how you got here!" he demanded, laughing and nervous at the same time.

She told him everything since she met Saidi on the street the day before in Zanzibar Town. He just shook his head in disbelief and smiled delightedly.

"It's so wonderful I can hardly believe it! I was trying to find some way to get you off the Island. There hasn't been any way at all to get that 56,000 shillings. And now you're right here beside me. It seems unbelievable."

Melissa moved closer to him and put her hand lightly on his arm. "I'm here and I'm never going back without you." She spoke softly, but there was no mistaking the firmness of her resolve.

"Yes. Where we go from now on, we go together."

He put his free arm around her shoulder and pulled her close. "I didn't bring you a dress. I was in a hurry to get out here, but I did bring along a big towel – it's in the back seat."

Melissa turned around, reached for the towel and draped it over her shoulders.

Tonio said, "My friend, Mrs. Gomes, has a daughter about your age and size. She is studying in Scotland and Mrs. Gomes is all alone. I know she will be glad to lend you her daughter's tropical clothing and you can stay there, too."

Traffic keeps left in East Africa and steering wheels are on the right hand side of the car so Tonio drove into town with his right hand on the wheel and his left around her shoulder. Every so often he pulled her even closer, and squeezed her arm so hard she knew she would have bruises, but she didn't mind. There were few cars on the road into town; now and then Africans on foot, several on bicycles and a little boy herding a few goats. Melissa watched the passing scenery and said, "It seems unreal – and yet we are actually together and this is Tanzania!"

"Yes, let's stop here and get caught up on news before we take you to Mrs. Gomes' apartment."

"No, please." Melissa laughed, "I feel embarrassed to be dressed like this in the city. Also, I think I won't feel safe till I am indoors somewhere – can you understand?"

"Of course I can," he agreed gently. "I know how you feel; everything is going so fast. We will be at Mrs. Gomes' home in a couple of minutes. I've often thought that it would be an ideal place for a girl escaping from Zanzibar, or anyone fleeing anything, I suppose. It belongs to a Rubén Gomes. Several of his relatives and other Goans have apartments there. People are continually coming and going. Visitors often stay from UK or Kenya. People will just assume you are someone's cousin or sister-in-law."

"Do you think Tanzania might try and return me to Zanzibar?"

"I suppose it is possible. But I don't think there is any reason to suspect you came from there. I doubt that Tanzania tries very hard to find Zanzibari girls to send back—although the two places are legally one country now. It is Zanzibar that passed the law that unmarried women have to pay to leave the island.

Why should Tanzania try to enforce it? But then, who can say?"

"Mrs. Gomes doesn't know I'm here, does she?"

"No, not yet, but she and I have often talked about you coming here and she always said you could stay with her until we were married, so I know you will be welcome."

Melissa felt ridiculous walking up the stairs in the Gomes building wearing a bathing suit and a towel. The halls seemed full of people, doors opened and closed continually and children ran in and out. Everyone smiled and nodded at Tonio and if they all wondered where he'd found the bathing beauty, at least no one asked.

He knocked firmly on the door with a sign that read, 'Mrs. Imelda Gomes' and soon a voice called out, "Who is it?"

Tonio answered triumphantly, "Tonio and Melissa!"

A short, plump woman in a dark, printed sari opened the door and exclaimed, "Tonio and Melissa!" Tonio gave Melissa a gentle push ahead of him into the flat and closed the door behind him.

*Beautiful Indian girls in the their best Sari's strolling
to the Azania Front Park for the usual Sunday evening
gathering. The brother of one of them is "in charge".
(Circa 1969)*

CHAPTER TWO

"Yes, it really is Melissa." Tonio said triumphantly. "She just arrived and doesn't have anything with her but what you see. I hope you can take her in and lend her some clothes?"

"You know I can!" she assured him while giving Melissa a warm embrace.

"Come with me, my dear. I'll show you your room and find you something comfortable to wear."

The bedroom had a huge wooden wardrobe against one wall. "Use anything in there that you want." Mrs. Gomes said as she pointed at the wooden monster that held her daughter's clothing. "I think she even left some sandals. Yes, here they are. I hope they fit. If not, just curl your toes in them a little for today. Tomorrow we can buy you a smaller pair."

Melissa felt grateful to find such a wonderful refuge. Mrs. Gomes was saying, "The bathroom is here – I'll start the shower for you so you can wash off the salt. You did come by dhow, didn't you?"

"Yes, it doesn't seem possible that I am here."

Melissa was in a hurry to rejoin Tonio so she quickly showered off the salt and started searching for things that looked like they might fit. Everything was a bit too large, but a sari can be wound to fit anyone and she found a pale green sari blouse that was only a little too big. She combed her wet hair into a rope and pinned it securely on top of her head with hairpins she found on the dresser. She looked older and less like a refugee.

She caught the expression of pleasure on Tonio's face as he watched her come into the room where the other two sat talking.

Mrs. Gomes saw them looking at each other so lovingly that she laughed and said, "For heaven's sake, go for a drive or something. And come back later and I will have a good meal ready for you to celebrate Melissa's arrival."

Melissa didn't feel ill at ease with her hostess who was a motherly type, but she wanted to be alone with Tonio. They had so much to talk about and plan for, and she knew that he wanted to be alone with her, too. They left the flat and went out to the little car. His hand in hers felt big and strong and it made her tremble just to feel it in her own. She had wanted to be with him for so long.

"I'll take you down Ocean Road. It's very beautiful. I used to think about driving there with you, especially when I saw other couples going for a drive. I was always so lonely and I felt left out. I didn't want to go out with the other young men because they were interested in meeting girls and I already had my girl, she was on Zanzibar.

Tonio pointed out the sights along the way and Melissa enjoyed the view of the ocean, the modern homes and embassies, but most of all she enjoyed knowing she was with the man she loved.

He parked the car facing the sea. In the distance,

too far to see, was Zanzibar. She stroked his wavy black hair and saw herself reflected in his eyes. They had planned to talk so much, but instead they said very little and were content just to sit wrapped in love and in each others' arms.

Finally Melissa said rather shyly, "Tonio, I'm very hungry. Is it about time to go back?"

"Oh, I'm sorry. What have you had to eat today?"

"A banana." she said with a sigh.

After dinner they went for a walk on the beach. The beauty of the tropical night, being together again after two long years and so much fear for her, made it a night they would never forget.

People in love have a special awareness. Love may be blind, but certainly not to everything. The stars of two hemispheres shone bright in the inky black sky. The breezes felt softer and the reflection of lights on the water were more beautiful.

The street by the sea was crowded with people out for their usual Sunday night stroll. Most were Asians. All the women were wearing colored saris, like so many brightly colored birds. Girls attracted the glances of the young men while giving the young men smiles and furtive glances. Their mothers walked nearby keeping a watchful eye on romances and chatted happily with friends.

The men talked together and the children ran about and seemed to be constantly eating something. Several Africans had set up stands where they sold oranges, slices of fresh pineapple and bags of popcorn. There was even an ice cream cart making the rounds, the tinkling of its little bell brought crowds of children running up with their treat money.

The lights from the ships in the harbor, and the street lights along the shore were all reflected in the water. The palms were dark lace against the sky and the diamond nose rings and glittering gold bangles of the Hindu women flashed in the artificial light.

There were Sunni Muslim women in black buibui robes and a sprinkling of Bohora Muslim women in blue robes. Well dressed Sikh men with their sari or kurtoo clad wives mixed here and there with a European couple who had come out to enjoy the passing parade and in doing so had become part of it.

Tonio greeted acquaintances, but no one stopped to talk with him so there was no need for introductions. Just as well, because they hadn't been able to think of any good way to explain her presence.

As the hours passed, it seemed as though the two years they hadn't seen each other amounted to only a day or two.

Melissa was back at the Gomes flat by eleven, but she was exhausted and fell asleep as soon as she lay down. She didn't awaken till the other tenants began to stir at six the next morning.

Every effort was made to let breezes flow through all buildings because of the intense heat. So noise and cooking odors were freely exchanged as well. In the back courtyard, servants were busy cooking up a huge pot of ugali, the corn porridge that is the staff of life in Tanzania.

It seemed to her that she must be the only person in the building who wasn't busy. She got up and looked through the wardrobe for a dress and found a white piqué that wasn't too dressy and slipped it on. She wasn't used to wearing so short a dress, but a short dress made her look more like a University student home from the UK.

"What do you plan to do today, Melissa?" Mrs. Gomes asked after their papaya, toast and tea.

"I don't know. It depends on what Tonio can find out at his office. If he can discover some way for me to stay in the country legally, now that I am here, we will just marry."

"I hate to discourage you, my dear. It certainly may be possible, but you must keep in mind that the Island authorities may ask Tanzania to send you back."

"I know. It is probably a risk for Tonio even to ask the questions of the immigration department, so he said he will ask a black friend to do it for him."

"Probably a good idea." Mrs. Gomes said with a sigh.

"I thought of going to the Canadian Embassy – I didn't mention it to Tonio and I wasn't sure until this very moment talking with you. I need to face the fact that I can't be both happy and frightened at the same time. I think I will go and see if it would be possible for us to live in Canada...maybe I can have something good to tell Tonio this noon..."

"I don't see what harm there can be in asking at the Canadian Embassy. I'm sure they won't do anything to harm you, and you can always say you are asking on behalf of a friend. If you would like me to come along, I'd be glad to."

"It would be wonderful if you came with me. I don't even know where it is!"

"We'll walk over to Dewhurst's Grocery and find a cab around there." Several children and their ayahs made room for them to pass on the steps. The street outside was crowded and busy too. A taka taka lorry, or trash lorry, stopped to collect refuse and Melissa and Mrs. Gomes picked their way cautiously around it.

"Whew! That was close!" Melissa exclaimed after she'd dodged a bicycle just in time to avoid getting run down by a driver who couldn't have been less concerned about his near accident. "He didn't care at all!" Melissa sputtered angrily.

"No. He probably didn't. Some tribal people are not fully convinced that people of other tribes are really human, so how do you suppose Asians and Europeans must seem to them?" She answered her own question. "Probably not quite real."

"He seemed real enough to me!" Melissa answered indignantly.

"Yes, but you have lived among people of other races all your life. He has probably gone from a society that was very primitive to one where he drives a car. Perhaps all in the space of a few weeks. He will change, but in the meantime, we have to hope we don't get run down!"

Melissa was still sputtering, half to herself and half to Imelda Gomes who was hailing a cab. At the white flag with the red maple leaf of the Canadian Embassy, she paid the driver and told him not to wait. They entered the building and went straight to the receptionist where Melissa said, "I would like to speak to someone about emigrating to Canada."

The woman pressed a button on her desk saying, "I will see if Mr. Dixon is free." An answering buzz came through and she said, "Yes, you may go right in. First door to the right."

She left her friend paging through a Maclean's Magazine and hurried into the office. Mr. Dixon was so pleasant and welcoming that she was immediately at ease. He looked rumpled, as though he had slept in his clothes. His shirt sleeves were rolled up and his sandy hair kept falling over his glasses making it necessary for him to jerk his head from time to time in order to see properly.

She explained her plight truthfully and waited to hear his reply while he toyed with his pencil and made his peculiar little head shake to clear a lock of hair away from his glasses.

He sighed, and said slowly and regretfully. "I'm sorry, Miss. There just isn't any way you can enter Canada legally without a visa, and you can't get a visa without a tax clearance and you can't get a tax clearance in Tanzania as a Zanzibari unless you have permission to leave the Island."

"And I can't get that without paying 56,000 shillings." Melissa finished his sentence for him.

"Yes." The Canadian was obviously distressed; his hair had fallen back onto his glasses and it took two of his nervous jerks to clear his vision.

Melissa stood up, pushed her chair back and said, "Thank you, anyway." to the embarrassed official who'd hurried around his cluttered desk to open the door for her. She hated to admit to herself how much she had counted on being able to go to Canada. Mrs. Gomes put down her magazine and joined her.

Neither of them spoke as they walked down the hall. Finally, the older woman read her face and knew that the answer must have been a final 'no.'

"Don't worry. That was just the first stop, there will be other ways and one of them will work. Often we don't get what we want and then something better turns up. Let's go to the Arlecchino Ice Cream Parlor and have something cold and good."

"How could I get along without you?" Melissa asked seriously.

"Fine, no doubt. But you probably are better off with me than without me, and that makes me happy."

The Arlecchino was doing good business. As soon as one of the very tall African waiters ambled over, Mrs. Gomes ordered lemon squash for herself and chocolate ice cream for Melissa. They sat at the only vacant table under a fan that tried to churn up the air enough to provide a bit of cool air on a day when the temperature was we ll into the 90s. "This is lovely ice cream. Here I am—a girl without a country and no prospects of having one, and I'm eating ice cream and enjoying it just as though I had good sense!"

"Might as well. How would it help anything to pass up ice cream?" Mrs. Gomes asked reasonably.

They hadn't been at the flat long when they heard

Antonio call at the door. Melissa nearly flew to meet him. His whole face seemed to light up when he saw her. She reached for both his hands and drew him inside the flat. When he noticed that their hostess was not in view, he took advantage and gave Melissa a lingering kiss. Finally he asked, "What did you do this morning?"

"We went to the Canadian Embassy and I was told, 'No tax clearance, no visa, no Canada'."

"I would have expected that." Tonio said. "On my lunch break this morning I talked with a fellow who had some good ideas."

While the three of them had lunch, Tonio outlined the new plan and it turned out to be as illegal as it was simple. He intended to buy her a passport from a printer. Melissa looked quizzically from one to the other, and her friend said, "I don't see why not—after all, she is from Zanzibar!" Imelda Gomes was well past questioning the legality of things if they seemed moral to her. The matter appeared to be settled.

Tonio picked her up after work and they drove over to a large bookstore which was also a printing and engraving business. There were several people in the main part of the shop browsing through paperback books in Swahili, French, English and Italian, buying stationery, pencils, pens—the usual merchandise of such places.

They walked to the back of the shop where unopened stocks of books and paper were kept. There were several small offices off it, no more than cubicles really. In one of them a woman was perusing sample invitations and printed stationery. She looked up momentarily and went back to making her selection.

The next office was empty except for the man behind the desk. Tonio went in, explained his business and then motioned for Melissa to join them. The casual onlooker would probably suppose that this was an engaged couple come to select wedding invitations. There was certainly nothing sinister about the little glassed-in office, nor the man who was greeting Melissa in a friendly but businesslike way.

"Yes, I see your problem. I think we can have you suited in two or three days time. We shall need the fingerprints of the young lady, a small passport photo—both of which I am prepared to take care of right here. The fee for this passport service is rather high. There are, as I'm sure you understand, various risks involved. We need to have regulation passport books which someone must supply us. Those people must be paid. Then the cost of the very skilled labor – however, I am sure you understand that 2000 shillings is not unreasonable?"

"That's fine. I will pay you when you have the passport ready." Tonio looked happy.

"We always collect on delivery – in cash to avoid what might be the nuisance of cashing checks."

"I can well imagine." Tonio said, trying not to smile at the solemn way the affair was going.

"Now, if I understand you correctly, you are interested in just one passport, a Tanzanian one for the young lady? Why do you not consider providing yourself with a couple others as safeguards? We will be happy to supply you with Indian passports, and British also. One never knows when the need may arise. We have several satisfied customers who believe that three passports are a basic minimum in these troubled times."

Melissa had a fleeting imaginary picture of several pompous businessmen all giving testimonials to the absolute need of having citizenship in three different continents all at the same time.

Tonio answered this with a final sounding, "No, this will be plenty."

The man led Melissa into another room which had photographic equipment in it. He wrote down her birth date, age, height and weight. He seated her on a bench, tilted her head slightly and took passport photos.

In the meantime, Tonio gazed thoughtfully around the tiny office which was decorated with at least a dozen colorful calendars from as many countries.

A loud noise from the bookstore intruded on his calendar gazing. Someone must have accidentally knocked over a bookcase full of books. He half rose from his chair to see who that unfortunate might be. He heard other loud crashes and saw that Tanzanian officials had entered the store and were knocking over displays of books. They had arrested the man behind the cash register whom Tonio knew as one of the proprietors.

Tonio ran to the other side of the room, took out Melissa's application and two others that caught his eye. He shoved them into his pants pocket and ran back to the room where she was having her photos made. He grabbed her by the arm and said, "Police are raiding the shop – is there a back entrance?"

The photographer ran past Tonio and called back, "No!" He was going to destroy what records he could before the police got to him, but it was too late. He was arrested as soon as he entered the outer office.

Tonio pushed Melissa towards the office where earlier they'd seen a woman selecting stationery. There was no one in there now so they sat and began to page nervously through the samples. They had scarcely started when a policeman came in and pushed over the shelves.

"What's going on?" Tonio asks with as much surprise as he could summon.

"Go along now, this shop is closed." the policeman said brusquely.

Melissa and Tonio walked quickly out of the store. A guard stood at the door and from his sullen demeanor they had no doubt that he would have enjoyed arresting them just for something to do. He didn't speak, just gave them each a solid shove in the rear with the butt of his rifle and then they were out in the bright sunshine again.

CHAPTER THREE

"Tonio, what do you think will happen when they find my application in his office?"

"They won't. I grabbed it before I went back to get you. Did they take your picture?"

"No, but he does have my fingerprints."

"Let that be a lesson to you." he said with a reassuring smile. "Don't rob a bank here since they have your fingerprints. Of course, who knows whose they are. Well, so much for the shady side of the law. My first effort to buy one little passport and I had to be where they raid the place. Think of all the satisfied customers who feel that 'in these troubled times...'" and she repeated with him. "'Three passports are a basic minimum.'"

For the next few days the newspapers carried long accounts of the Government's case against the Shanti Brothers, Printers. Melissa and Tonio were not the only ones who read the papers closely wondering if any of the customers of the shop would be prosecuted. Apparently the Government was only holding the proprietors for the offense of transporting money out of the country illegally. She could relax.

The hope of buying a passport was dead. In countries like Tanzania, finding a printer is no easy task and finding one who is both skilled and honest and most important – one who has connections with people able to steal passports – best forget the idea.

Dar es Salaam was different from Zanzibar Town, but not so different that she couldn't enjoy the simple pleasures of walks by the sea, drives with Tonio, the occasional movie. There had been such a dry period since her parents died that just feeling free to move about and not worry about how to get off Zanzibar made life quite pleasant.

One of the best features of the block of flats where she lived was that someone was always moving in or out, and this made things safer for her. Most of the tenants were Goans and some had lived on Zanzibar before the revolution.

One of the young men looked vaguely familiar to her. She thought he was staring at her once when they passed in the hallway, and yet he always nodded politely and never spoke so she guessed she had been mistaken.

Soon after the raid on the printers, there was a farewell party for a young Goan couple who were leaving for California and everyone in the building was invited. The man had worked for the US Embassy in Dar for several years, and his wish to emigrate became a reality when he was sponsored by his retiring supervisor for a job in California.

When Melissa had an opportunity, she said quietly to the bride to be, "Please tell me how you managed to get a passport."

"I arrived before the 56,000 shilling insanity. So we have Tanzanian passports. The US Government is giving us visas and we will become US citizens as soon as we possibly can." She looked thoughtfully at Melissa and said hesitatingly, "I suppose that you came from Zanzibar illegally and can't find work, can't leave, and can't even get married?"

"Something like that."

"If I were in your position, I would write my old school in Zanzibar and have them send my records to a school of some kind here in Dar. I would send to my parish for a copy of my baptismal record and have it sent to a church here. School and church records are often used as proof of citizenship since most people never have any need for a passport and only apply for one when it is needed."

"I'll try that!"

"I wish you good fortune!"

The next morning Mrs. Gomes was going shopping so Melissa went along with her and mailed her requests for records. It would hardly be safe to have them mailed to her directly so she asked that they be sent to the pastor of the church Tonio attended.

"I hope they forward your records immediately, Melissa. I enjoy your company so much, but I know you are anxious..." Here her voice trailed off as she stood face to face with a familiar young man who was grinning broadly. She looked perplexed. He asked, "Melissa is leaving us so soon?"

This was the same man that Melissa had seen in the building and wondered about. Now there was no doubt. Something about his oily smile, oily hair and even oily pointy-toed shoes struck Melissa as utterly repugnant so with a light '*Kwa heri*' for farewell, she walked past him with Mrs. Gomes close behind her.

"Do you know him from Zanzibar? He has been here for several years – and yet he seemed so-oh, I don't know. So chummy with you, as if he were enjoying some secret joke. His name is Bruno Benavides."

"Yes, I heard people calling him Bruno at the party, but I doubt I ever saw him on Zanzibar."

Tonio's office was not many blocks from the Gomes flat and Melissa expected him soon after four. Five o'clock came and went and still no sign of him. They made some lemon squash and were drinking it on the veranda when finally Tonio drove up.

Melissa waved and sighed with relief, "I don't know why, but I felt worried. He is always here soon after work."

Tonio's usual two at a time on the stairs was now more like an over-weight man in his fifties. Melissa poured a glass of the cold drink and took it along as she went to answer his knock at the door.

"Does that drink look good," He took her by the hand as they walked out to the veranda where he sat down and wiped his forehead and neck with his handkerchief, but his shirt was soaked and sweat was running in rivulets down the back of his legs.

"Warm day." commented Mrs. Gomes, "But I would think you would be reasonably comfortable in your short sleeved shirt, short pants and knee socks!" She looked ruefully at her own body swathed in layers of sari material.

"Normally not bad," Tonio agreed, "My office faces the sea and I get a good breeze." He sighed and then asked, "Melissa do you remember the Benavides family?"

"No. I was just going to ask you if you did." Melissa answered with surprise.

Mrs. Gomes added, "I know the family to say 'jambo' and 'kwa heri' to them. I have known who Bruno is for some time. He thinks he is quite a ladies' man, and he often has a pretty girl riding behind him on his piki piki. A Honda, I think it is. Always a different girl."

"Bruno was waiting for me after work today. He insisted that I walk over to the harbor with him because he said there was something I ought to see. At anchor is a ship bound for Zanzibar in two days. Bruno was so friendly that you'd think we were the oldest and best of chums. He pointed to the ship and said, "It would be a great shame if Melissa had to be aboard, so I asked him what he was getting at and he said, 'I think 5,000 shillings will be about right. After all, it is much cheaper than the 56,000 shilling and she is already here.'"

Melissa asked bleakly, "Do you think he will tell if you don't give him the money?"

"I think so. There seems to be a lot of malice in that man – he was not only blackmailing me, he was enjoying the power he had over us even more."

Mrs. Gomes broke in with, "Do you think he would stop at 5,000 or do you think he'd keep coming back for more? He used to work off and on at Shanti's. But now he seems to be *retired*."

"Certainly, he'd keep coming back for more. If he worked at Shanti's, he probably knows several people who pay him to keep his mouth shut. That's the problem with doing anything outside the law. No matter how crazy the law is. I think the man who ran Shanti's considered making false passports a business, much like engraving wedding invitations. A bit more risky, but much more lucrative. To Bruno, it's blackmail opportunities." Tonio swirled his drink around and looked disgusted.

Melissa said heatedly, "It is shocking to me that he is a Goan, born and schooled on Zanzibar, just like us. I want to be able to trust our own people." Her eyes filled with tears and she ran sobbing from the veranda.

Neither of them followed her. Mrs. Gomes looked sadly at Tonio and shook her head in disbelief, not at Melissa but at the cruelty of Bruno Benavides. Finally she asked, "When did he say you have to pay him?"

"Two days from now, before that ship sails. I could give him the 5,000 but that is all I have. There just wouldn't be anything for a second installment, and I'm sure he would turn her in finally. I'd love to wipe that self-satisfied grin off his face." He pounded the chair arm for emphasis.

Mrs. Gomes said calmly, "You could put Melissa on the train tomorrow night and she would be in Mwanza by the next day and then you would have time to think of some plan. The problem now is that time is against you."

"I don't want to send her to Mwanza...this is a big city, there she would be more obvious. What is to prevent Bruno from watching the train departures? He scarcely has to move from his own rooms to see the trains come and go. I think he would consider the possibility of her going away by train."

"I suppose you're right. He can spend his time on that noisy piki piki of his going from the bus station to the train depot and back again. There aren't many departures."

She got up from her chair to see about Melissa. A gentle knock on the bedroom door brought Melissa's voice saying, "Oh, come right in. I'm almost ready." She was arranging her hair and seemed to have her emotions well under control. "Please excuse the outburst, I was so upset – what I'd like to do isn't legal, or moral, but the crying fit seemed to have helped."

Tonio welcomed Melissa back with a smile and said, "Let's go out for a walk, the heat is dying down now and it is pleasant."

As they walked down Independence Avenue, Tonio said suddenly, "Melissa, let's go see Father Ciprian. He knows his way around as well as any man in the country. He might have some ideas."

They walked the few blocks from the Avenue to the Cathedral Church. It was imposing in its setting by the sea, behind a lovely park-like garden, to the side of it a large Catholic school, a convent and a home for the White Fathers – called that because of their white habits. Next to the church were offices where the priests took care of pastoral business. Melissa and Tonio walked up the open outdoor staircase and sat down on a bench to wait for the door to Father Ciprian's office to open.

They hadn't long to wait. A tall, bearded priest came out to the veranda. "Why Antonio, who is your friend? I think this is the first time I have seen you with a young lady!"

They both stood up and Tonio said, "Melissa, this is a good friend of mine, Father Ciprian. Father, this is my fiancée, Melissa Lopes."

"Come into my office. There is a ceiling fan and I think it is doing a better job for the moment than the breeze." Inside he motioned them to chairs in front of his desk. The overhead fan worked mightily, churning the heavy warm air around.

"I will get right to the point of our visit and hope you will be able to help us think of something we can do. Melissa fled Zanzibar by dhow because we had no hope of raising the money to get her off legally. She has been staying with Imelda Gomes. We tried to buy her a passport so she could remain here. We were in Shanti's offices trying to do just that when the business was raided and closed down."

"Bad business, that. Were you questioned?" The priest asked anxiously.

"Oh no. They thought we were choosing wedding invitations. They didn't actually ask, just saw us looking through a book of samples. The next idea was to send to Zanzibar for records which will be sent to you." The priest nodded and Tonio went on, "She hoped to get a passport on the strength of pretending that she had been in Dar since before the 56,000 shilling rule went into effect."

"Yes, I believe that might work."

"We thought so, but Bruno Benavides overheard Mrs. Gomes saying to Melissa that she would miss her when she left, but knew how anxious she was."

Father Ciprian looked startled at this bit of information, seemed to be thinking it over and then asked, "Was your father the Lopes who had a shop in the heart of Zanzibar Town and also several coconut plantations?"

"Yes. My father was Ricardo Lopes...did you know him?"

"I only saw him a few times. I know who he was and I know what kind of man he was. I am going to tell you something that may explain Bruno's actions. His father was entrusted with the collection and care of a very large amount of money for the building of a new church. Benavides was a respected businessman with various interest both on Zanzibar and Pemba. It seems his clove plantations were in trouble of some kind, and he used the church funds. A short time later, the bishop asked for a complete accounting and the shortage was exposed.

Bruno's father was never prosecuted. Ricardo Lopes, who was his friend, paid back a large portion of it and pleaded with church authorities on Benavides' behalf. Benavides then came to Tanzania where he died not many years later. He was a thoroughly embittered man. He blamed your father for his troubles, saying that if Ricardo Lopes had paid the full amount then he, Benavides, could have stayed on Zanzibar and recovered his losses. Instead he had to sell out in disgrace and start over with almost nothing in Tanzania."

"But that's ridiculous! It wasn't my father's fault."

"Oh, I agree. But Benavides was a complex man. He had been very rich. He lost everything. It was too hard for him to admit that it was his fault and that he owed your father for paying a large part back and keeping him out of jail."

"Doesn't Bruno know the true story?" Tonio asked.

"Yes, I'm sure his father told Bruno that he had intended to repay and only needed the church funds for a few days – something of that order, probably. And he probably did intend to repay. Do you think Bruno might tell the police Melissa is here?"

"I am sure of it. Today after work he threatened to tell the authorities if I don't have 5,000 shillings for him by the time the Baraka sails for Zanzibar."

"When is that?"

"Two days."

"Are you going to pay him?"

"No. I know better than that. I was so angry I could scarcely talk. I think he believes I will have the money for him."

"Perhaps Melissa can eventually get the passport on the strength of her records, but that takes time." They could all hear the large office clock ticking away time as they sat in that small office. Then Father asked abruptly, "Do you follow race car rallies?"

Tonio laughed ruefully, and said, "Well, I guess I do at that. Before the East African race the rally fever gets most of us, I suppose. Why do you ask?"

"Because I wonder if you know Harry Richards, an Englishman who works at the airport. Very keen on racing. Drives like a madman, even in town, unfortunately. Still, he is supposed to be an excellent driver. Going to drive with Ahmad as his second in the Peugeot. I was talking to Richards on the street just this afternoon and he said that he and his wife are driving to Nairobi tomorrow to feel out the track, so to speak. I think you might ask him to take Melissa along as their little girl's nursemaid."

"I've heard of Richards, but I don't know him. If you think we might ask him, we certainly will!"

"Nice chap, actually. Bit different, to be sure. I remember when they first moved into their flat. I went over to visit the family and saw a little girl walking along the edge of the roof – it is four floors up. Harry was not a bit worried. He felt it would teach her balance. The mother is much the same. Fortunately, for my peace of mind, the child soon tired of roof-walking and went off to play with her cat. She talks to the cat in Kikuyu because her first nursemaid was Kikuyu and she gave her the cat."

Tonio jotted down the directions to Richard's flat, they thanked the priest and hurried over to the Gomes flat to pick up Tonio's car for the drive out to call on the rally driver.

The Richards family lived in a block of flats that

had been constructed by the Tanzanian Government to house professional workers. The buildings were four stories high, modern in design and extremely spacious. But the climb to the fourth floor seemed a bit much to Melissa who was wearing a sari and wishing she weren't. As an ideal garment for stair climbing, the sari doesn't make the grade.

The noise coming from the fourth floor was startling. A man's voice roared angrily, *'I'll kill you'* and other equally violent threats. They hardly knew whether or not to ring the bell. They decided they should because they might prevent murder.

The doorbell sounded just once and the door was opened by a short, freckled Englishman who invited them in very graciously and showed them to chairs near a window over-looking a golf course. He didn't seem in the least bit surprised to see them, nor curious about their visit. It was much as if they dropped in regularly.

Richards looked cool in a short sleeved shirt open at the neck from which a mat of curly red hair could be seen. His legs and arms were also covered with curly reddish hair. He was slightly shorter than Melissa, so his head came to Tonio's chin.

A little girl came in, smiled at everyone and waited to find out who they were and what they wanted. A woman's voice called from a bedroom saying, "I'm going to have an early night, love. See you in the morning."

"Sleep well, love." Harry answered.

Tonio spoke first, "Pardon our intrusion, Mr. Richards, but Father Ciprian suggested that you might be able to help us."

"I don't know whether I can or not, but Father Ciprian is a friend of mine and I will try."

Tonio explained the situation in the briefest terms possible, leaving out anything that might arouse the little girl's curiosity too much, but giving Richards to understand that Melissa had to find refuge for two or three weeks outside Dar and there were passport difficulties.

The Englishman read between the lines and asked only one clarifying question, "Zanzibar?"

For once, Melissa herself answered. "Yes," she sighed.

"Father Ciprian is probably right and you should come with us. We will be leaving tomorrow early, be in Nairobi tomorrow night. Do you have any place to stay?"

"I have an uncle there. My only living relatives are my uncle and his family, and a cousin and her husband on Zanzibar."

"Be here at the flat tomorrow morning at seven. Bring a thermos of tea or water and some lunch. We don't plan to stop much and I don't think my wife has extra on hand because we planned to be out of town." With that he led the way to the door and said cheerily, "Don't worry."

They thanked him and started down the stairs accompanied by the little girl. She was taking her cat to stay with the neighbors while she was out of town. She talked to the cat in Kikuyu just as Father Ciprian had said she did, but she talked to them in Swahili.

After she left them, Melissa remarked, "That certainly is a strange little English girl. I wonder if she speaks English?"

"I suppose she does. I wonder who her father was threatening to kill? He didn't seem angry when he opened the door and there wasn't anyone in the flat to threaten the girl. He was getting ready for bed. I'm glad you have a way to Nairobi, but I wish it was someone a bit more ordinary."

It was obvious to both of them that Tonio couldn't take Melissa to Nairobi himself, if he lost his job they would both be in worse straits than they already were. Still, they had felt so confident that they'd never have to leave each other and now it was off into the unknown. Melissa seemed less upset than Tonio. By then they were near the sea and Tonio parked the car so they could sit on a bench and watch the Indian Ocean. There is little more comforting than seeing the waves lap against the shore, the foam on the water, the occasional leaping of a fish and the moonlight streaming into the dark water turning part of it into a river of light.

She broke the silence with, "Don't worry so much. I am not discouraged. After all, I am off the Island, I am with you now and I will soon be with my uncle and his family. I haven't seen him in years, but I remember him well. Then too, we have a hope of a quick solution when my records come in, and well, it will all be fine."

Her sweet little face looked up at him so lovingly

that without considering where they were, he took her tenderly in his arms and kissed her hair, her cheeks and lingeringly, her lips. Melissa held him tightly to her and felt warm and loved.

Three African women in buibuis held the tops of the black robes to cover their mouths, but there were slip-ups as they commented eagerly to one another while trotting behind their husband. He was dressed in a long white kansu and wore an embroidered skull cap. He carried a highly carved ebony walking stick in one hand and a rolled-up umbrella in the other. When he saw Melissa and Tonio kissing, he was clearly shocked to see such goings on. His wives giggled nervously and had to increase their pace to keep up to him.

Melissa started to giggle just like the African's wives. Tonio looked at her in surprise and then laughed aloud. They were mildly embarrassed, too, but they arrived at the Gomes apartment in good humor.

"Did you have a nice evening?" Mrs. Gomes asked hopefully when they came in.

They told her of the plan for Melissa to leave for Nairobi in the morning with the Richards family, and then visit her uncle there until her records came.

"What about papers at the border?"

"They often don't bother to check, you are supposed to register within twenty-four hours of arrival. If they do check, the Richards have papers and will just say she is their nursemaid."

"Won't they have to account for her when they leave?"

"Not if she isn't traveling on his passport and she won't be. Of course, she can't go to work there and she can't return alone legally either until we get some papers for her here and send them on to her. She is supposed to be at Richards' flat at seven, so I'll come by for her at six and we'll go out and have breakfast."

"No, much safer to eat here and take a lunch from this kitchen. So, you come here and have your breakfast with her and then take her to Richards. We'll see you at six tomorrow morning!"

It was still completely dark after their breakfast as Tonio drove through the quiet streets to the car park in front of Richards' flat. He took out his wallet and gave Melissa ten one hundred shilling notes and some change for soft drinks and phone calls. She felt embarrassed but didn't refuse the money because she knew she needed it.

The askari who was guarding the building came over to see who was in the car and what they wanted. He was carrying a sharp, dangerous looking panga that glowed and glinted in the artificial light. He seemed reassured when he recognize the same couple he had seen with Richard's daughter the night before. Tonio talked to him softly in Swahili. The guard was tired from the effort it takes to stay awake all night and anxious for the sun to come up so he could take his panga and torch and go home.

CHAPTER FOUR

S oon the Richards family came down loaded with three suitcases, a large picnic basket and a huge thermos. Tonio helped them all get settled, wished them a good trip, kissed Melissa and went off to buy a newspaper to read while waiting for the government offices to open. He was aware of real misgivings, but relieved that Melissa had a place to go and people to take her there.

Melissa sat in the back seat with the little girl who turned out to be completely tri-lingual. She spoke un-accented English just as any child of five might do in Merry Old England. She seemed to prefer to chat with Melissa in Swahili who felt a bond with this little blond child because she herself spoke Swahili most of the time too when she was a child.

The Richards proved to be great company. They knew all sorts of songs which they sang with gusto as they raced down the road. The car didn't have good shock absorbers or perhaps they had been shocked too much and all four passengers were thrown about even when the road wasn't bad. It didn't bother the Richards at all. They jounced happily over every pothole.

Harry Richards turned around and roared at Melissa, "The reason the car makes so much noise is that the muffler is shot. I'm going to give it a decent burial in Nairobi when I get a new one."

Mrs. Richards kept track of really bad spots in the road, and the mileage between places and jotted it all down in a notebook. She and her husband had dozens of fascinating tales to tell. They had to yell over the noise, but they didn't seem to feel the strain. Melissa found herself enjoying the day. She hadn't ever been to a city the size of Nairobi and found herself looking forward to seeing her Uncle and his family. Kathy entertained with stories about what she thought was the eccentric behavior of the teachers at Dar es Salaam Nursery School.

Richards and his wife had changed places. He was sleeping peacefully in the cramped front seat while his wife drove as furiously as he had. Both were skillful and quick-reacting which Melissa hoped would compensate for their reckless abandon at the wheel. Kathy had fallen asleep with her curly blond head on Melissa's lap and the warm damp weight of the sleeping child was lulling her to sleep too. She rested her head on the back of the seat and hoped they wouldn't hit an elephant broadside.

She woke with a start when the car swerved, made a strange sound and screeched to a halt. Kathy sat up sleepily and asked what happened. Her father rubbed his eyes and said sleepily as he yawned and stretched, "That was a blow-out."

"Mm, yes, 'twas," agreed his wife.

"Where are we now, then?" asked Harry pleasantly.

"I make it about five miles from the first Masai boma."

"Good job we have a spare," Richards said as he got out and started hunting for the jack. He let out a string of epithets, insults mainly to a friend who had last borrowed his car. Melissa was quite upset. If the unflappable Richards was that concerned, they must be in real trouble.

Kathy noticed Melissa wringing her hands and said, "Don't mind Daddy. He always yells like that, but he never even swats me."

Mrs. Richards got out and helped her husband rummage through everything, but finally admitted defeat. "It just isn't here. Nothing for it but to have lunch and hope someone comes by soon."

She took out the picnic things and Melissa added what Mrs. Gomes had sent and they had a lunch of sandwiches, mangoes, hot tea and samosas with a large, warm, sticky but delicious English chocolate bar which they shared for dessert.

No one came along the road, the sun was high in the sky and it was getting almost unbearably hot out in the open. Melissa was glad it was daytime because it was obviously good lion country and she didn't like to think of a hungry lioness coming on them and deciding that people would make a nice dietary change.

Mrs. Richards was a great mystery story fan, so she opened her luggage and took out three paperbacks for them to read and Kathy got her coloring book and they all sat down in a grassy spot near the road to read and wait for help.

Kathy tired of coloring and settled herself down in the back seat of the car for a nap. The other three tried to get interested in the mystery novels, but it was so hot and uncomfortable they simply couldn't. Melissa noticed with a start of surprise that in spite of the heat Richards teeth were chattering. His wife looked at him in alarm and said, "Is it?"

"Fraid so," he answered. Fiona felt his forehead and said, "Best get you back in the car."

Richards rose slowly from his seated position on the sun-baked ground. He was shivering violently.

Melissa didn't have to ask what was the matter with him. "I have some chloroquine tablets in my purse, I'll get them." She hurried back to the car and took out the aspirins and the anti-malarial pills Mrs. Gomes had packed for her and gave two of each to the sick man, along with a thermos cup of water.

Two hours or so passed without any passer-by at all. The two women looked down the road from time to time but nothing appeared. Finally, Fiona exclaimed, "Ah, Masai – herding cattle this way!"

"Are you sure?"

"This is Masai country, the last village of any kind that we saw was a Masai boma – if only they were Kikuyu or any of the Swahili speaking people. I don't happen to have a word of their language."

Soon the dust cloud was very large and close. It was obvious that it was Masai herding their hump-backed cows. Melissa felt afraid, but didn't confess her fear to Fiona who was acting as usual, interested, but not worried.

Finally they were surrounded by cattle, by dust and by Masai who looked at them with unconcealed curiosity. Two of them were peering into the car and calling out information about what they saw there.

Suddenly there was a great roar from Richards who opened the car door, throwing the herder who was leaning on it off balance, and surprising everyone else into staring at him and at Kathy who woke up and started whimpering. Richards was flailing about wildly, threatening to kill all the bloody Nazis. It was frightening to watch him. His wife and Melissa realized he was raving with malaria and quite out of his mind, but they had no way of communicating to the herdsman who stood back from the wild man and raised their spears to protect themselves.

"No, no!" gasped Melissa, "He will be impaled on their spears!" She and Fiona ran to him and tried to hold his arms and quiet him. He pushed them off as easily as he might brush off two annoying flies. But he seemed to understand that he shouldn't charge into all those raised spears so he didn't attack, but continued to yell and threaten.

Kathy was now crying piteously. Her eyes were as wild with terror as her father's were with fever. Fiona touched one of the Masai and pointed to her husband and began to act out a pantomime. She chattered her teeth, shivered violently, felt her head and indicated pain and then looked imploringly at the men who had been torn between watching her pantomime and keeping an eye on her husband.

A murmur of sound rose from the herders who understood that Fiona was acting out 'malaria.' Whether it was as common in Masai lands as on the coast, she didn't know, but felt sure that some of them must have experienced it.

One of the men made a tying motion with his hands; he seemed to want rope or something to tie Richards up with.

Fiona didn't know if she ought to give this nomadic stranger rope to tie up her own husband, but she couldn't very well let him hurt himself, and the state he was in, it was obvious she and Melissa couldn't handle him. She got a length of rope out of the boot of the car and the Masai she handed it to called out directions to the others. Two of them held Richards from behind and the two others tied his arms together. They looked inquiringly at the car and Fiona pointed to the ruined tire, hoping they would understand. One of them did, and explained something to the others who seemed to be pondering a course of action.

They finally agreed on a plan, and some grinned and others laughed aloud.

Richards was still raving. Kathy still whimpering. Fiona went to her daughter and said,

"Not to worry, Daddy is just raving from malaria, but he will be better in a day or so. We have him tied up so he won't get hurt, that's all."

The Masai indicated by pointing and nudging that all four were to go with them. Fiona said, "Thank you for your hospitality, gentlemen, but I believe we are well suited right here."

Naturally, none of them understood a word she said and they prodded and pushed the travelers in the opposite direction from where they had last seen a village. They hadn't gone more than a few hundred yards when they saw another Masai boma. The children and some of the women came out to see what was going on. All were interested in the unexpected visitors. The chief emerged from his dark hut, rubbing his eyes and stretching. He was accompanied by several of his wives. Although old, shrunken and withered, he was obviously the chief by the deference shown him by the others and by the old British army jacket he had donned to greet the visitors. It looked unbearably hot, but he probably thought it added a formal touch, and it did.

His wives ranged in age from grandmothers to a young girl about Melissa's age. The young wife was lovely, with a tall, slim body, elegant carriage and fine, graceful features. She was bare from the waist up but wore many strands of copper coil around her neck which extended almost to mid-chest. Around her waist she'd wrapped a length of bark cloth. Several rows of copper wire encircled her slender ankles. Her head had been shaved bare. She was very interested in Melissa and looked at her with undisguised curiosity, but she smiled so warmly that Melissa smiled and nodded pleasantly at her, too.

The herdsmen who had brought them explained about Richards to the chief, who gave several orders. They were led to a dwelling that was to be the 'guest house.'

Fiona had brought along the picnic basket and Melissa had the extra thermos so they weren't worried about food.

The young Masai wife followed along after them, and when they were in the guest hut she said what must have been, 'I'll go and get you a nice lunch.' She wasn't gone long and on returning she had two gourds with her which she indicated were for their use. They looked at her blankly as she took one to her mouth and drank, wiped her mouth delicately and then took a sip from the other. Meantime, several of the men had taken it upon themselves to get poor Richards down onto a bed of skins. He was exhausted from his exertions and didn't offer any real resistance. Once he was securely tied down, one of them raised Harry's head up and offered him a gourd full of something. He seemed to be coming out of his wild imaginings or perhaps he was just too tired to fight. He took a sip and then was gently let down onto his bed of skins and mats.

When her hostess passed the gourd to her, Melissa smiled as politely as she could but didn't try to drink, then passed it to Fiona who nodded her thanks as ceremoniously as one might do having tea with the Queen. She raised it to her lips, drank, and without so much as a grimace handed it back to the Masai girl. She in turn, asked some questions and pointed at Kathy. Fiona touched the thermos that Melissa had in her hand. The child was about to refuse, but Melissa said softly, "Unless I am mistaken, Kathy, those gourds contain blood and milk. The milk is warm, the gourd has been washed out in cows' urine – it smells very strong. It probably won't hurt you, but don't you think it would be nicer to drink this tea?" Kathy reached for the thermos cup and for the first time in her life she drank tea with something like eagerness.

Their hostess scurried around arranging three more beds of cow hides, for which they thanked her. It was going to be completely dark very soon. There really wasn't a thing to do but get a good night's sleep and hope for better luck tomorrow.

"Well, at least Bruno would never think to look for me here!" Melissa said to no one in particular. She got out two more malaria tablets, two aspirin and more water which she gave to Richards who seemed to be almost himself again. They were afraid to let him loose, and since he didn't ask to be untied, they let well enough alone.

Melissa, Fiona and Kathy made a rather large bed of the three smaller beds their thoughtful hostess had provided and lay down with Kathy in the middle to try to get some rest.

Kathy liked a nice bedtime story and her mother obliged by telling one. The bedtime story seemed incongruous in a place where the smell of cows' urine permeated everything. Not only the hides on which they lay, but the air itself, the walls of the hut, everything bespoke the Masai dependence on cattle.

They were awakened in the morning by the lowing of cattle and perhaps even more by the biting of some ferocious big black flies. Richards seemed to be his normal self. He still complained of a great headache and said he felt weak as a kitten, but he was more than ready to be untied.

"Do you have anything left to eat in the picnic basket I see there in the corner?"

"Not much," said Fiona. "There is a bit of cheese, a samosa or two and some cold tea."

"Sounds delicious," her husband said with gusto. "Let's share it out, and I could do with a couple of aspirin and some chloroquine if there is more." Melissa got him the pills, which were washed down with a bit of the leftover tea. "Going to have to get back to the car, you know." he sighed. "Hope it is still there and in one piece."

A great deal of noise and excited conversation outside the hut attracted their attention. Kathy ran out to see what was going on.

"Someone just came in a Land Rover. Oh, is he big!"

The two women and a still very shaky and weak Richards went out into the bright sunlight shading their eyes to see, after the darkness of the windowless dwelling. Near the Land Rover was one of the biggest men Melissa had ever seen. He called out a greeting to the Masai who all seemed delighted to see him. He slapped several on the back, shook hands solemnly with the chief and when he saw the Richards and Melissa, he laughed aloud and started in their direction followed by several of the Masai who also seemed to think it was funny to have so many outlandish guests at one time.

"Whatever are you doing here?" boomed the big white man whose face wore a look of utter astonishment. "Was that your car I saw abandoned on the road? I got out and looked in it and around it to see if there was anyone who needed help."

"Yes, that's our car," said Harry. "Got a flat, no jack and yesterday I had malaria something awful, thought the Masai were Nazis and the Masai had to tie me up. This is my wife, Fiona, our friend, Melissa Lopes and our daughter Kathy. We're on our way to Nairobi. I'm going to drive the Peugeot in the rally and I wanted to note problems on the track. Never really expected the ones I found, but then, one never does."

The big man laughed and agreed with that philosophy. "I'm Doc Hayes, I work for USAID. I come to all these bomas regularly. We are trying to help upgrade the Masai herds and we're having real success stamping out rinderpest."

"We're glad to meet you, Doctor. I don't suppose you have any extra malaria medicine with you?"

"I've a few extra pills, but I am not the kind of doctor you think I am. I'm a veterinarian; started out life as a cowboy on the American range."

The chief who had been standing near the big American, gave a few orders and soon everyone was seated on the ground and several women went back and forth carrying gourds full of milk and cows' blood.

"The chief here is always amazed at how little I eat, considering I'm such a big guy, but I never really worked up much of a taste for the cuisine." Nevertheless, the Doctor took a couple healthy swigs from the gourd when it was offered, smacked his lips politely and passed the thing to Richards who was certainly not going to be outdone guts and he drank even more deeply.

Harry wiped his mouth with his hand and said gratefully, "Thank heaven, it was the one with milk in it."

"I generally bring along some cheese and canned meat, but it's been a long haul – I'm on my way back to Dar and a few days rest now."

"I hope you have a jack I can use on my car?" Harry asked hopefully.

"Oh, I'm sure we can rig up something. I have a kit for patching tires too. We can get you going right now or you can stick around and watch the big cattle dip. The boys here have planned a big one—we are going to run every one of the cows through. Gets rid of the fly that causes rinderpest. These fellows are A-1 cattlemen, but when they first start using the dip, I like to be around to be sure that none of the animals are left out...source of re-infection. The Masai have names for each of their animals; they have so many words to describe cows that sometimes it's only possible to describe a certain kind of horn by using the Masai word. I show them how to do something, and if they understand the reason for it, I can count on them doing it.

"They really love cows. They aren't only their source of food and shelter, they seem to be a way of life. Why, I've seen them turn down a gift of newly shot hardibeast or wildebeest. The women sometimes ask to have the stomach of the animal, makes a nice container, but they don't care for meat. Just milk and blood."

"I'll feel better when I know the car is ready to roll. Can we get it fixed before the cattle dip?" For answer the veterinarian just got up and motioned for Harry to follow him.

The car was soon ready to go but they all wanted to stay and watch the cattle dip. It was a truly spectacular affair with huge herds of cattle, clouds of dust, swarms of flies and so much skill and strength were required that it was much like watching a sports event.

"I wish I had something to give these people," Fiona said regretfully as they prepared to leave. I suppose we can leave the picnic basket and thermos. It should be left with the chief." Fiona took the empty picnic basket, and Melissa her empty thermos and they walked over to the chief and ceremoniously left the gifts in front of him.

He made a short speech which they thought must have been, "Oh you needn't have bothered," smiled at them and ordered one of his wives to take the gifts inside. They waved farewell to Doctor Hayes and the Masai and were on their way again.

"There it is," Richards roared triumphantly several hours later as the outskirts of the city of Nairobi became visible.

Melissa was unimpressed. On either side of the road she saw desperately poor African dwellings, too close together, too many dogs, here and there a scrawny chicken and an occasional goat. She felt disappointed but continued to watch intently as the car moved more slowly now. As the outskirts were passed, new and beautiful homes appeared, prosperous businesses, and well-tended gardens.

The downtown area was more modern than Dar and much more prosperous. It reminded her of European or American cities she had seen in movies, except that here most of the people were black with a good sprinkling of Asians and just an occasional European.

"Is it always so noisy?" asked Melissa over the roar of the car motor.

"Sometimes worse," answered Harry cheerfully.

Melissa pondered anew how hard it was for her to understand why people enjoyed noise and traffic snarls.

"I don't know my way around here well. I plan to drive to the New Stanley Hotel. We will all get cleaned up, have dinner, and then you call your uncle and find out how to get to his house. I'll drive you over."

Melissa was glad that she wouldn't have to appear in her dirty sari, with her hair all tangled and so full of dust that her comb refused to go through it.

The hotel was no longer the largest and best in town but it was elegance itself to Melissa. Everything seemed the last word in modernity. The Richards took two adjoining rooms and Melissa sighed with pleasure at the luxury of the air conditioned lift to the second floor.

Kathy went right to the window to see the city spread out before her. The little girl was so engrossed in the scene below her that Melissa knew she would be content there while she herself took a much needed shower. She had never felt so thoroughly gritty before. The water ran off her in reddish-brown streams, carrying away the dust of the road and the Masai cattle dip. She washed her hair and combed it into one long thick and shiny rope that fell almost to her waist. She put on a clean cotton dress and then called to Kathy.

"Come on in, I am going to give you the best bath of your life and make your hair shine like sunshine."

"No, thank you, I'm not really very dirty," the little girl said seriously. Melissa restrained a laugh. Kathy's yellow curls were now a medium brown, her face was only clean where streaks of perspiration or tears had washed it and her clothes were thick enough with dirt to literally stand alone.

"Oh come now, Kathy," Melissa coaxed, "We all want to be clean enough to eat in the dining room of this beautiful hotel. How would it be if they told us we were too dirty to be served in public and would have to eat in our rooms?"

Kathy had a good bit of self respect as Melissa had long ago discovered. This got her into the bathroom where Melissa bathed and shampooed her until her friends could recognize her.

Kathy was quite pleased to feel clean and nicely dressed again and she was just beginning to complain that it was always so long between meals lately, when the Richards called at the door to say they were on their way to the dining room and to come right down.

After a fine meal, Melissa went to her room, sat on the bed and looked up her uncle's phone number. She found it easily, but once again she felt full of doubt—fearful that her uncle and family couldn't take her in perhaps, and then what would she do? Where could she go when the Richards had to return? She had been pretending this was a holiday, that she was traveling with friends and would soon visit her uncle and family. As she dialed the number, she knew it wasn't true. She was fleeing from the Island of Zanzibar and all that it had become for her. She was escaping from a blackmailer in Tanzania and if the authorities in either Tanzania or Kenya were to learn of her presence she might well be fleeing from them, too. The phone at the other end only rang twice when it was answered by a servant speaking English with a soft African accent.

"Yes, Mem Sahib, I will call Mr. Lopes to the phone."

A short pause then, "Lopes here."

"It's Melissa, Uncle. I am in Nairobi!"

"Melissa! Where are you calling from?" Her uncle sounded delighted to hear her and his voice was so like her father's that when a smile came to her lips, her heart seemed to feel it too and stopped its awful pounding against her ribs.

"I am at the New Stanley Hotel—I came to Nairobi with some friends of a priest. He's also a friend of

Tonio Da Silva. I thought perhaps I could stay with you until some arrangements have been made in Dar Es Salaam." She realized that she had put that badly. After all, he was her father's only brother, but it had been some time since she'd seen him and she felt reluctant to impose.

"Of course you must stay here, Melissa. I'll be right down to collect you. In about half an hour, go down to the lobby and I will meet you there."

Melissa knocked on the Richards' door and told them the good news. Harry said he wanted to go downstairs with her and meet her uncle and see if he had any ideas about passports and such, but Melissa knew it was just his way of seeing if her uncle looked like a responsible person.

When the hotel doors opened to let in Mr. Lopes, Melissa knew at once who he was. She rose to greet him and he welcomed her in an excited mixture of English and Portuguese. Melissa felt relieved to see him and eager to introduce this fine looking gentleman to her English friends.

After the introductions, her uncle asked, "Did you have a good journey?"

Melissa was thinking of an answer to that when she was amazed to hear Harry say,

"Well, yes, we did, rather."

Her uncle was telling Harry where he lived and inviting the Richards to his home next evening for dinner.

"No, thank you kindly, but we have so many things to see to that we must decline. But while you are here, I would be interested to know if you have any ideas on how we can get a Tanzanian passport for Melissa—she left Zanzibar by dhow."

"No I haven't, but then I've not given it any thought. I didn't know she wanted to leave the Island. I could have sent the money to buy her way out. Perhaps there is some way still – anyway, she is here now and safe. I can always give anyone who is over-curious the idea that she is visiting from Mombasa."

Melissa spoke softly to Harry Richards, "Thank you for everything, I wonder if I shall ever see you again. I've never known a family like yours. I hate to lose you."

"Nonsense" Harry assured her, "you will be back in Dar in no time and we will be running into you all the time."

"Come now, Melissa, your aunt and cousins are very anxious to see you and I said we would return soon."

Melissa's uncle led her out to the car park where he unlocked a black Mercedes, helped her into it and put her little suitcase in the back seat.

"Mmm, this is certainly more comfortable than what I am used to, and quieter." She amused her uncle by telling him how the Richards roared above the sound of the engine, how they took everything in stride and were such interesting company.

"They are very kind and helpful, aren't they?"

"Yes, Uncle, they are – and they are very brave too. I'll tell you sometime all about my adventures with them. If you don't believe a word of it, I won't blame you. It all seems kind of unreal to me now."

Her uncle pointed out places on the way, especially Uhuru Park. "My children like to come here to listen to bands at night and chat with friends, you will like it, too. Our house is not far now."

When he turned into the driveway of a large Tudor style home, Melissa was impressed. "It looks like something out an English novel."

"Yes, because Zanzibar architectural style is not suited to Nairobi, it really gets quite cold here. We even have a fireplace and electric heaters."

The long driveway was bordered by flowers and the house encircled with well-tended shrubbery. There was a wide lawn and two tables with umbrellas and several chairs.

No sooner had the car door closed, than the rest of the family hurried out to meet her. Her aunt was a pleasant looking woman of about forty five and the two girls were in their late teens. The other cousin was a young man in his early twenties. They all began to ask questions at once as they crowded around her.

"Let her come in and have a cup of tea, there is time for everything." her aunt said protectively. "She looks bewildered by all your questions!"

Melissa was surprised at the dim interior, so much less open than houses in Zanzibar or Dar. She said, "I feel that I am on a stage set, that this can't really be me here in this lovely house, but then I look around and you all look familiar from pictures you've sent...I wish I could have brought you some snapshots of my cousin and her husband to show you," Melissa said wistfully.

A cup of tea and little cakes were set on a table near Melissa's chair and then her cousin George said, "We are all anxious to know how you manged to get off Zanzibar, none of us knew you wanted to leave!"

Melissa told them exactly how it happened and explained that she hadn't told anyone because she didn't feel it was right to pay ransom and that it would have bothered her to have them pay it for her. She didn't explain that Tonio had been trying to save it, because she knew that would sound pathetic and no one likes to feel pathetic.

"I don't know this Mrs. Gomes you speak of who is so good to you, and I have never heard of Father Ciprian, but I was a good friend of Tonio Da Silva's father. I knew his mother well, too. They are fine people."

"They are both dead now, Uncle." she said as gently as she could.

"So many old friends are gone," her uncle said sadly. "I would like to help Antonio if I can. Has he a good position?"

"Yes, he is a senior auditor with the government, his work is interesting and he has Tanzanian citizenship, so perhaps he can continue there."

Her uncle nodded, "Yes that is possible, Nyerere is a reasonable and practical president – but he has some advisors who aren't...and there are other political forces..." Obviously he wasn't too sure that Tanzania would continue to be safe.

Melissa then told about Bruno Benavides and his

threat. The whole family seemed shocked into silence. Finally her uncle said, "I knew his family, too. If it were not for my brother—your father, Melissa, old Benavides would have been in jail. Your father helped him by replacing a large part of what he had stolen from church funds. In return, the Benavides family showed no gratitude, they seemed to hate all of us after that. You help some people, and then they accuse you of not doing enough, of being arrogant."

"Tonio told me that Bruno acted as though he enjoyed frightening us, he likes the idea of the money, but the power is important, too."

"Shocking, shocking. But Bruno can be forgotten for now, Melissa. You are out of his reach. I don't suppose he knows you have relatives in Nairobi and even if he does, he can't do a thing."

CHAPTER FIVE

When her uncle returned from his shop the next afternoon, he was a bit less sure of Melissa's safety. He had asked around and friends told him that the government in Kenya was quite strict in requiring all foreigners to register with the immigration office twenty-four hours after arrival...deportation to be immediate if the regulation is not complied with.

"But I believe you will be safe if you stay close to home."

Melissa agreed to do so, but wished she had been cautious enough to do that earlier. That very morning, her cousin George invited her to come along with him to the godown where the goods were kept. He told her that his father had suggested she have some dresses made by his sisters' seamstress and she might as well choose the materials since he had business at the godown and she could come along.

She was thrilled by the prospect of new clothes that were really her own. She hadn't had a new dress for a very long time and the ones she had now belonged to someone else. How like her uncle to realize she needed things of her own. He was like her father in more than appearance.

Melissa thought about what had happened at the godown that morning, but decided that such things probably happened often and not to worry. The building was full of bolts and bales of materials, some of coarse quality and others like spun gold. The new things from India looked to her like something out of Aladdin's adventures. Silk sari fabric with gold or silver borders in lovely designs, satins, cloth of gold...

"Choose what you want from bales and bolts that are already opened, the ones that are still closed are to be transshipped from here to various stores around the country."

Melissa gave a little skip of delight. George laughed at her affectionately. "I have business to attend to, I'll come back and collect you when I've finished, so don't wander off."

There were several fundis (workers) in the godown, carrying in bales of goods or carrying them out. Melissa asked one of them if he would please bring her scissors and a tape measure so she could cut off a few dress lengths of material. He didn't understand English and shook his head, so she asked him in Swahili which he understood although she had heard him speaking what she thought must be Kikuyu with the other workers.

The worker was helpful and brought the things she asked for as well as a clean piece of muslin so she could spread the goods on the floor while she cut the seven yard lengths needed for saris and the two to four yard pieces for modern western style dresses.

"You are from Mombasa, Mem Sahib?" the fundi asked in a conversational way.

Melissa almost answered, 'Hapana, Bwana.' (no sir) but she realized she would have to pretend she hadn't heard the question or she'd have to lie. So she asked instead if he would please bring the pink and gold sari material and replace the bolts she had already taken material from.

Mombasa Swahili and Zanzibar Swahili are alike, the rest of the coast speaks the language with a slightly different accent. Naturally, he thinks I'm from Mombasa, she told herself. He recognized that my Swahili is different, he isn't suspicious, just friendly. Besides, why would he care?

Her thoughts were interrupted by angry shouts, "Haven't you got the lorry unloaded yet? Do you think you get paid to sleep all day? I am fed up with your slow work!" It was George scolding the African who had been so helpful to her. She was shocked. George had seemed so mild mannered. The African turned abruptly to leave but Melissa had seen the expression on his face—undisguised hatred.

She looked up at George and was confused to see him looking at her pleasantly just as though nothing had happened. She finished folding the last cut of material and the piece of muslin and stood up ready to go, her hands were trembling. Her own expression must have been quizzical because he said offhandedly, "I pride myself on having good fundis. I didn't realize he was helping you, but not to worry, he probably missed many a good scolding and this makes up for it. They are like children, you know."

Melissa didn't argue with him but she did wonder if the African couldn't say the same thing about George and perhaps with more justification.

Now, just a few hours later, George was telling his father about their trip to the godown and about Melissa choosing fabrics. She was pleased with her uncle's reaction, he smiled happily at her pleasure. Her aunt said they'd have a seamstress come right to the house and get to work on Melissa's new clothes. The cousins looked at her affectionately, and then to her surprise, Melissa felt tears flowing down her cheeks.

The mood was lifted by George who said teasingly, "All the struggle on Zanzibar, the troubles in Dar and when do you cry? Why, when everything is fine!"

Melissa had to smile at the truth of his remark and said, "I must be over-tired, please excuse me, I'll go up to bed now."

"Good night" called her aunt and "Sleep well" ordered her uncle.

"Good night" she replied and started up the stairs, then half turned to look at the family. The girls were playing a game, her aunt was crocheting, her uncle and George were reading and the radio was playing modern music. It was the very picture of happy home life. She felt grateful to have found safety while she waited for the papers that would allow her to return to Tanzania and marry Tonio.

Melissa's bedroom had a private bath adjoining it, so she took her nightgown and went in to shower. The bedroom was at the front of the house, but she hadn't drawn the draperies. She had no need for light because the moon was full and beautiful and she enjoyed seeing it from her bed.

She turned the shower on full force and talked to

herself sternly as she bathed, "I am grateful they are so good and that they can afford to help me. Uncle knows this country and is influential, he will find a way to get legal status for me somewhere with Tonio." She recited these thoughts out loud and was startled to hear herself adding, "Lord have mercy," just as she would have done if she were reciting a litany in church. "I really must be tired and nervous, I'll sleep and in the morning I'll feel cheerful."

With that good advice to herself she turned off the shower, dried herself and slipped into the nightie. Goodness, someone must have a terrible program on, and it's way too loud, she thought.

But no, that was Clara's cry, a shout from George, an agonized wail from her aunt and then the sound of bare feet running all over – bare feet running up the stairs. She turned off the bathroom light, locked the door and hardly dared to breathe.

A man's excited voice called out in Swahili "How many in the family?"

And an answer, "Five. We have them all here." The voice of the second man sounded vaguely familiar, then the bedroom door was flung open and someone was in her room—the bathroom doorknob turned, but it was locked and didn't open. She was fearful that her breathing might be heard, but the intruder left as quickly as he had come.

There was more shouting downstairs, but no words that she could recognize and then the front door slammed and she sensed that all had left. Almost in a trance, she opened the bathroom door and went to her bedroom window in time to see six or eight men with pangas and knives scatter in all directions as they reached the street.

Mustering every bit of courage she could summon, Melissa grabbed the robe her aunt had given her and still barefooted, she ran downstairs.

The living room was total horror, her uncle's body was as usual, sitting in a chair, but his head was unrecognizable. George's head was hardly part of his body, the girls and her aunt had obviously been stabbed to death. Blood was everywhere. Bare feet had tracked through it and puddles of it were on the sofa and on the stairs.

She ran upstairs and fell on her bed sick with horror and shock. A numbness seemed to start in her fingers and toes and spread to her arms and legs. "I should call the doctor—no. They are dead!"

She got up to call the police and then stopped, "No. I am here illegally, they will think I had something to do with the murders. At best I would be sent back to Tanzania, and then to Zanzibar, or I could be sent to jail here. No, I must run away from here. I can't help them," She began to sob great horrified sobs of outrage and fear, but even so, she dressed quickly, took a suitcase and packed it with simple clothing, and then taking her purse, she ran down the stairs out of the house, forcing herself not to look again at the bloody scene in the lounge. She knew it was already engraved in her memory and would be there until the day she died.

When she reached the street, she walked as quickly as she could towards the Pan Afrique Hotel, the closest public place she could think of that would be open.

The clerk at the reception desk looked up and asked, "May I be of service, Miss?"

"First, I need to know when the next train departs for Mombasa." She asked on impulse and realized that might be the answer. Mombasa is on the sea, and perhaps if she had to, she could get away again by dhow. She wouldn't be noticed in Mombasa because there are many Asians from India there and even her Swahili would blend in better.

The clerk was looking at her in a puzzled way, "Are you alone, Miss?"

"Only for the time being," she said, forcing herself to smile.

The clerk gave her a knowing grin and she realized he thought she was eloping. A reasonable guess on his part because well dressed, respectable looking Asian girls don't show up alone at hotels at 11 pm. Rather than correct his mistake, she decided to take advantage of it. She gave him a big smile in return. She knew she was trembling again and an elopement would explain her nervous state. Again she forced back the horrible memory of her uncle's family in the home she'd just left.

The clerk made a phone call for her and said, "There is a train to Mombasa tomorrow morning, would you like a room here for tonight?"

"No, I can't wait until tomorrow – do you know if there is a plane yet tonight?" She asked the question and then tried to think whether she had enough money for a ticket.

The clerk said he would ask and called the airport for her. "Yes, there is one leaving in an hour!" He looked quizzically at her for further instructions.

"Please ask them to reserve a seat on it for me."

"What name, Miss?"

She almost blurted out her own name and then checked herself in time and said, "Mary Martines."

He winked at her and said, "That's a nice name." Obviously he didn't believe that was her name, but he made a reservation on the flight for her and called a taxi. He was so cheerful about what he thought was helping Cupid that Melissa almost asked him if she would need any identification. She thought better of it, and decided she need not concern herself with that since she would still be within Kenya. She might be asked for some identification for other reasons though, and she certainly hadn't any. She could go back to the house and get more money and a cousin's ID But she knew she wouldn't willingly set foot in that house ever again.

Another alternative came to her mind. The Richards! Maybe they were at the New Stanley Hotel. She would phone and see if they might possibly still be there.

"Do you have any public telephones?"

"Yes, Miss. Over by the magazines."

Melissa left her suitcase by the desk and hurried into the phone booth to look up the number of the hotel. She asked for the Richards' room, half sure that he would have left the city.

"One moment, please," said the operator and she heard the phone ringing. She prayed that he would be in and just as she was about to give up, the clerk said,

"Oh here they are. They've just come in. I'll ask Mr. Richards to take the call here."

In a moment she heard Harry's voice, then her own saying, "Can I see you right away? Something terrible has happened." She nearly screamed remembering, but forced her voice down.

"Of course, where are you?"

She told him and said a cab had been ordered and she would see him soon. She hung up, she couldn't say another word.

The clerk was looking interested and puzzled although he hadn't heard the conversation.

"Thank you, you have been very kind." she said calmly.

"Glad to be of service. Have a nice flight."

The taxi arrived, she could see its lights through the glass in the entrance door. For greeting the driver asked, "Kiwanja na ndege, Mem Sahib?" (*Airport Madame?*)

"Hapana, Bwana. Hoteli New Stanley." (*No, Sir. The New Stanley Hotel*)

The driver looked surprised but didn't complain. When they pulled up at the New Stanley, she paid him the exact fare and added only a customary tip. She didn't want to do anything that might call attention to herself or anything that he might remember and wonder about later.

Harry Richards was sitting facing the door while he waited for her. Fiona must have gone up to check on Kathy as soon as the two of them came back. "What happened?" Harry asked as he took her suitcase.

"Let's sit in that far corner where we can be alone," Melissa suggested. They walked in silence to the other side of the reception and found two chairs apart from all the others.

She told him what had happened as calmly as she could. Twice she had to stop, once to lower her voice because she wanted to scream, and once because she thought she was going to faint. She lowered her head to pretend to tie her sandals.

Richards looked horrified and said, "Oh my God!"

"Should I go on to Mombasa? There is a flight out in about half an hour. I have a seat reserved under the name Mary Martines. I don't want to get you into any trouble."

Instead of answering, he asked, "Who do you think did it and do you know why?"

"I don't know anything except what I told you. Shall I try to get that plane?"

"No. I don't think so. It is probably too late already for you to catch it. You stay here in Kathy's room tonight. We were planning to return to Dar tomorrow and I think you had best come with us."

"Will I put you in danger just being with you?"

"Oh no, everything will be fine," Richards assured her in a rather distracted way as though he were trying to make some sense out of what she had said and plan ahead at the same time. "You are trembling, are you feeling all right?"

"I don't know. I just can't say how I feel, it's so..."

"No, I suppose you really don't know, it isn't every day...Thank God. Let's go up now. I'll give you a tranquilizer."

Richards took her suitcase and told the clerk at the reception desk that his child's nursemaid had returned and would be sharing his daughter's room.

Mrs. Richards was sitting up in bed reading one of her more gory mystery stories, if the cover on it was any indication of its contents. She was surprised to see Melissa and her eyes grew huge with amazement as Richards told her the story while Melissa sat on the bed and heard it all again like a nightmare retold.

"Have you notified the authorities?" Fiona asked and then answered her own question. "No, of course not, you couldn't very well do that. Are you sure they're all dead?" Fiona asked, her brown eyes looking more piercing than ever.

"Yes," sobbed Melissa.

"Well now, well now..." Fiona was trying to put an everyday face on this as she did on every other disaster, but was finding it impossible.

"Oh yes, your tranquilizer!" Richards said to Melissa who was still shaking visibly. He went to the bathroom and returned with half a glassful of brown liquid. Melissa had expected a pill of some sort. She looked at the brownish drink and thought, 'Well, a man who has often had malaria and doesn't have chloroquine wouldn't really be likely to have tranquilizers.'

Aloud she asked, "Is it whiskey?"

"Yes, I put two little packets of sugar and a bit of hot water in with it so you can get it down. Drink it slowly, sip it if you can. Your stomach is probably nervous too, and we don't want you to be sick. Easy does it."

She didn't think much of the taste, but if it would help her calm down a bit she could drink it. Her own mind was in such turmoil that she was grateful just to follow Richards' advice. Fiona came around to the side of the bed she was sitting on and gently guided her into Kathy's room.

"Sleep here now. We'll call you. There is nothing you can do to help your uncle and his family. And nothing to be gained by going to the police and having to explain that you are here illegally. Even Mrs. Gomes and Tonio could be in trouble, not to mention your dhow captain. No. What one must do, one can do. You stay here and try to rest, even if you don't sleep. We'll only be going as far as Korogwe tomorrow, so it won't be a hard trip." Fiona's voice was firm and Melissa felt assured. If the Richards had become excited, Melissa knew she would have given in to hysteria. As it was, she accepted Fiona's belief that she owed it to others to calm down and rest.

CHAPTER SIX

Early next morning, Fiona said to her husband, as if she knew what he was thinking – and she probably did, "Not only that, love," she cautioned, "We must use a good bit of care ourselves. We have lived here for years, but in fact we are considered mere visitors. We can be asked to leave on twenty-four hours' notice at any time. I don't think it is unreasonable for them to have control over who enters and leaves Tanzania and Kenya. We certainly have stretched a few laws out of shape lately."

"We have that—but the alternative has always seemed so much worse."

"Yes, I'd do it all again, but it is wrong to let those poor servants go in all unaware and see such a terrible sight."

"Can't be helped. What bothers me is that Melissa thinks she might know one of the murderers, the voice was vaguely familiar, but she can't place it."

~

Harry's friend in Korogwe, Burt Jenkins, was delighted to see them and so was his wife who assured them that there was plenty of room for all. Harry explained Melissa's presence honestly, including the slaughter at her uncle's home.

"I know what you can do to inform the police," said Jenkins thoughtfully, "You can address an envelope to me, with a note that says six or eight men were seen leaving the scene of the crime carrying pangas and knives, and whatever else you know, and then leave it in the garage. I can mail it to the police saying that someone who passed through left it for me to send on, or I could send it with no explanation. That way you will have fulfilled your obligation to tell the police what little you know."

"Good. I'll do that."

Mrs. Jenkins took the others out to show them her vegetable garden. She had a large basket with her to fill with produce for them to take back to Dar.

Melissa walked along, feeling that she was standing apart, watching herself look at flowers, and seeing herself grow tired and warm and yet not really doing any of these things.

Fiona looked at her from time to time as if to say, *'You are doing just fine, keep moving, keep walking, talk when you can, smile if you can.'*

The noonday meal prepared by the Jenkins' servant was a fish, rice and coconut dish popular in East Africa. There was a fresh garden salad and sponge cake. Melissa ate everything she was served and once again it seemed she was watching someone else eat. She knew the food was good and that she should eat, but nothing seemed to have any taste.

After the meal, everyone went off to rest and Melissa dozed too until the sound of Kathy playing with a puppy aroused her. *'Well, what do I do now?'* she asked herself bitterly. *'I can't go to Nairobi and I am afraid to be in Dar. I won't go back to Zanzibar. I want to be with Tonio – if I could only get citizenship somewhere, then maybe we could finally be together.'*

In the next instant, she had a thought that spurred her to hurry out to talk to the others.

The two families were sitting in the lounge talking animatedly about rallies and mutual friends. "Ah, Melissa, come join us. I'll get you a glass of iced tea and some biscuits," Mrs. Jenkins said hospitably.

Melissa sat down next to Fiona on a sofa and said, "I just had a strange thought. It occurs to me that all my uncle's property would have been left to his wife and children, but they are dead, too! I am his only surviving relative! If he has a solicitor and I suppose he would need one for business reasons at least, won't they start looking for me? I will be nowhere to be found on Zanzibar and perhaps they will even think I must have been involved in the murders because I am the only one I know of who stands to gain anything!"

Jenkins reflected a bit and said, "I expect the authorities in Nairobi will try to get word to any remaining family. It would take some time to establish if there were any surviving members. It is possible that they have already notified Zanzibar. Yet I am inclined to believe that not much has been found out...perhaps by tomorrow."

"I agree," Harry said, "and if the cousins that Melissa lived with on Zanzibar are asked for her present address, they can honestly say they don't know."

"Isn't it possible that there will be the suspicion

that I had something to do with the murders?"

"No, I don't think so." Harry said thoughtfully. "It takes a certain mentality to commit heinous crimes and most humans aren't inclined that way."

"True, thank God" said Jenkins with a sigh. "When it is known that you are no longer living with your cousins, the authorities will think you have run away and probably found some way to leave Zanzibar. The money your uncle left, if it is true that you are his only remaining heir, will be put into escrow for you for a few years to see if you turn up. Much of his wealth will probably be taken by the nation in taxes."

Fiona suggested, "I think it would be well to have a good solicitor in Kenya looking after your interests, perhaps when you get back to Dar you can set Tonio to finding a good man to help you."

"Would that be very expensive?" Melissa asked.

"Not necessarily. He can be paid out of what you inherit, often a percentage of it. But you are not in any position to do it for yourself so a solicitor with a thorough knowledge of Kenyan and Tanzanian law seems indispensable."

The rest of the day passed quietly with visiting and making plans for the next rally. An early bedtime was decreed by Harry who wanted them all to be well rested.

Melissa went into her room armed with magazines to while away the time. Harry tried to make a phone call to Dar to find out what the situation was there. But the noise on the line was deafening. The operator kept trying to make the connection, but finally had to give up. There seemed to be no alternative, they would have to take Melissa back to Dar, no matter what. It seemed to Harry that Melissa needed to be with Tonio now – danger or no danger.

The trip from Korogwe was bumpy due to holes that had been made by the long rains and not yet repaired. Harry and Fiona took note of bad stretches and wrote down details they thought might help in the rally.

The Richards had timed the trip to include a leisurely picnic along the way, so that they would get to Dar just as it got dark.

"I think we should be as inconspicuous as possible. We will take Melissa home with us because no one would think to look for her at our place. It is possible that Benavides is trying to watch both Mrs. Gomes' and Tonio's places. I'll go to the Kilimanjaro hotel and make some phone calls when we get into town. Mainly to tell Tonio to come over but also I want to pick up the newspapers."

They arrived in Dar without incident and drove right to the flat because Harry said he was starving and wanted them to get started preparing something to eat while he made the calls.

"I can't think what we can make out of this," his wife said with a sigh as she surveyed the vegetables and eggs she'd brought from the Jenkins' house.

Melissa said, "I think maybe my mind is starting to work again, because I can think what we should do for a meal. If you'd like me to make a vegetable curry while you care for Kathy and shower and change, I believe I can do it in half an hour."

"Oh wonderful. I don't care what it is, we are all hungry, but I am so tired and my eyes hurt. I feel dusty inside and out."

Melissa put water on to boil the rice, fried an onion and added a large spoonful of Bombay curry powder, water and bits of chopped vegetables and let that simmer. Then she prepared hard boiled eggs, and cut up onion, tomatoes, a small bag full of cashews and a green pepper, putting each ingredient into a separate little dish and arranged on a tray. When the rice was done the vegetable curry could be poured over it and each person would choose chopped egg, onion, green pepper, tomato and cashews and add them to the top of the curry.

The heavy tramp of Richards' desert boots on the stair brought Melissa running to the door.

"I phoned Father Ciprian, he hasn't heard anything about you since you left town, and I didn't tell him about the murders. Just that we had to bring you back with us and that you would be staying with us for a while."

"Did you call Tonio?" Melissa asked.

"Yes, of course. I told him you were back with us, nothing more."

Melissa and the Richards were eating the hot meal, almost too tired to be aware of what it was, when Harry, without looking up from his food, said, "Ah, here comes Tonio."

Melissa went to the window. She hadn't been able to distinguish the sound of his car, but Harry was right. Tonio waved at her and ran up the stairs as fast as he could, by the fourth floor he was pretty well out of breath, but grinning broadly.

She held the door open for him and he picked her up and swung her around while he laughed and said delightedly, "Just couldn't stay away from me, could you!"

Fiona laughed and asked dryly, "Suffer a lot, do you, from a feeling of inferiority?"

"I am so glad to see you all, but how does it happen that Melissa is back here?"

"Sit down, have a cup of tea and we will tell you." Fiona said as she poured out a cup for him.

Harry sighed. "I'm too tired to be talkative, Melissa can fill you in on the trip down and back, but in broad outline – her uncle and his family were killed by a gang of house invaders that broke in night before last. Melissa was upstairs at the time and locked herself into a darkened bathroom. The others were killed by six or more men armed with pangas and knives. They thought they had all the family members, apparently. Then she came to our hotel. We spent last night in Korogwe, there was really no place to leave Melissa where her presence wouldn't stand out. So, here she is. She is going to sleep in Kathy's room for the time being. We have to make some plans. Nairobi wasn't the answer and I can't think of anything right now but how tired I am. Good night all." And Harry went to bed.

Tonio looked too stunned to comment. Kathy had long since fallen asleep with her head on the table.

Fiona carried her into the bedroom and said that she was going to bed, too. "Just leave the dishes. If there is anything I know for certain, I know that they will still be there in the morning."

"No, no," Tonio objected. "I'll help Melissa with the dishes and she can tell me everything. Thank you very much for all you have done for us. We certainly didn't think it would cause so much trouble for you."

"No trouble at all," answered Fiona sleepily as she shut her bedroom door.

Melissa told Tonio about the night at her uncle's house and her thought of going to Mombasa. "Do you think I should have gone there?"

"Certainly you did right in calling the Richards, but you were in such a state of shock I can see what made you think of Mombasa—the sea so you could hope to leave again by dhow if you had to and yet within Kenya so you wouldn't have to worry about border controls."

"I was glad that the Richards were still there. They have been so good to me. I don't even know if anyone has connected me with my uncle yet, we haven't seen the newspapers..."

"What are those newspapers on the bookcase, are they recent?" He walked over to the bookcase. "Yes, these are today's Standard of Nairobi and the Dar paper. Come here!"

Tonio pointed to a picture of a smiling family and Melissa said sadly, "Yes, that is my uncle and family...their home is in the background. I hope I never have to go into that place again. I can't get the picture of them as I last saw them out of my mind."

"I think you need a solicitor," Tonio said finally.

"You don't think anyone will suspect me, do you?"

"There wouldn't be any reason for that. Even if you were capable of it, which you aren't."

"The police might think so. I am their only blood relative."

"Unlikely that they would suspect you of a crime committed by knives and pangas. It boggles the mind to think that a whole family would sit quietly and let a young woman kill them one by one!"

"Yes, but do you think the police might believe I paid someone to do it?"

"No. I suppose you could hire killers in Nairobi or any large city if you knew the criminal class there. But murderers don't take out adverts in the Nairobi Standard so that young ladies can hire murder done in the same way that professors put notices in so people can make arrangements to study French. A girl new in town and alone couldn't do such a thing. Especially without money to pay the killers. Such arrangements aren't made on the hire purchase plan. We have to get you a good solicitor however."

"Then the whole story will be out!" Melissa protested. "I won't be able to get a passport through school records. Benavides will say you know where I am, and you will end up in jail." By now she was almost wailing, her voice was breaking and her spirits were as low as they had ever been. The horror in Nairobi had spurred her into action, but the idea of giving up on the passport and spending her life in semi-hiding was almost too much for her to bear.

"Melissa, don't cry. I'll keep in touch with the solicitor and I think that going through legal channels will be best for both of us. It isn't our fault we can't live on Zanzibar and you have to be somewhere. I am getting more than fed up with being at the mercy of scum like Benavides and afraid of custom officials, policemen, even border guards. I am going to find a solicitor first thing in the morning." His words were firm and decisive but his manner was gentle as he put his arms around her and pulled her to him. He stroked her hair and her cheeks and said, "Cheer up, you have been through so much, it won't hurt you to stay here and rest for a day or so. Don't leave the flat, though. Now go to bed and not to worry."

"Mmm" said Melissa, "That may not be easy."

"Well, what is easy in this life?" asked Tonio with a shrug of his shoulders for emphasis.

"You win. I won't worry. I'll just float with the current." she said, attempting cheer she didn't feel.

"I'll see you tomorrow. Stay in here." He kissed her again and held her close.

"Yes, I'll stay in here." she agreed and he left, this time taking the steps one at a time and slower.

CHAPTER SEVEN

Harry was up early and off to his job, and Fiona went grocery shopping after leaving Kathy at nursery school. Melissa saw her struggling along the road under the weight of two heavy grocery baskets. She felt guilty she couldn't go out and help her. When Fiona saw her at the window, she raised her hand and made a motion to stay back, as she shook her head in a decisive 'no.'

Melissa poured a glass of ice water to hand to Fiona as she came in. "Oh my, is it hot," Fiona groaned as she set the baskets down and flopped into the nearest chair.

"Here's the newspaper. I recognized your picture on the front of the Nairobi Standard so I bought a copy and now let's see what they have to say." She read aloud, "'Police are continuing their enquiries into the whereabouts of the niece of an Asian merchant who together with his family was murdered here three days ago. The niece was known to have been visiting at the time of the crime. The solicitor of the deceased gave police the information that the only known relative of Mr. Lopes was a niece who lived on Zanzibar. Island police have gone to the address supplied and have been informed by the girl's cousin that she disappeared from Zanzibar several weeks ago and has not been in contact with them. They did not fear foul play and have not reported the matter to island authorities. The police consider it likely that the niece from Zanzibar was visiting the Lopes family in Nairobi when the tragedy took place.

"Investigation is continuing, and the police are supplied with a school photo of the niece taken three years ago. If anyone knows the present address of this girl, he should immediately notify the police. Several persons are helping the police with their enquiries.'"

"The photo is rather blurred, but it looks like me. I suppose my cousins in Zanzibar didn't want to get me in trouble. They have several snapshots of me, many more recent than this one."

"Let's see, yes, you were younger, your hair was shorter, your face rounder, and of course, you don't wear a school uniform anymore. But it does look like you."

"Do you think that Benavides has told that Tonio knew I was here—or that Mrs. Gomes knew?"

"No. I think he sounds like someone who has his own financial interest at heart. He isn't exactly a public spirited citizen, you know."

"That's true enough. There wouldn't be anything in it for him. What he is interested in is money and revenge."

"Revenge!"

Then Melissa told the whole Benavides tale again, prompting Fiona to ask, "Ah, and the father's hatred was inherited by this son?"

"It seems so. He also wanted to make money on us, of course."

Fiona and Melissa exchanged newspapers and Melissa read the Dar Es Salaam account also which had substantially the same story as the Nairobi paper. Apparently no one in authority knew that Melissa had been in Dar before she was seen in Nairobi.

"It is ironic and sad, but now with the whole family gone, I probably will have the money to buy my way off Zanzibar."

"Inheritance is a slow thing. You may well never see that money at all. But even 'soon' is likely to be a matter of many months. Creditors will present bills, inheritance tax will take a very large slice and most people with the money to afford your uncle's home will not want to buy a house with such a history."

"Do you think the business can be sold?"

"I don't know, Melissa. Your uncle and his son ran it alone with only the help of laborers. Perhaps the solicitor Tonio finds could make arrangements to sell it."

There was a knock at the door then and Fiona motioned Melissa to go into one of the bedrooms before she answered it.

A middle aged man stood in the door way and said, "Good morning, I am John Mathers. Antonio da Silva spoke to me this morning about a problem a friend of his is experiencing and I thought I should come by at lunch time and see if I can be of service."

"Come right in, Mr. Mathers."

Fiona showed him to a chair and called Melissa to come out and meet the man that Tonio had engaged to help them.

Melissa was expecting a young Asian and was surprised to see a middle aged Englishman. She offered her hand to him as he rose to greet her.

"You have quite a problem, Miss. I am going to need your permission to handle the case. I have a form here which will empower me to act in your behalf, if that is your desire."

"Yes, I think so. Sometimes I wonder if I shouldn't just go to the authorities and tell them all I know and explain why I am here illegally and simply see what happens."

"Oh no! I don't think you should do that. It would unduly complicate your life, and, as I understand it, you already had a number of reverses."

Melissa marveled at the way he referred to the whole mess as a 'number of reverses.'

"What do you think the government here will do to me for leaving Zanzibar without payment of the 56,000 shillings?"

"Now that you are represented by counsel, I doubt that they will do anything at all. By the way, I am acquainted with the solicitor involved in your uncle's case."

"How did you find out who he was?"

"I phoned a friend in Nairobi and asked him who was the likely counsel for an Asian textile merchant and he gave me two names. The first one I called said he was handling the estate. I told him I would probably be in touch with him by phone later today, but at that time I didn't know if you would agree to have me handle your case."

"I am very happy to have you take charge of my affairs. You seem to know your way through this muddle. I hope there is some way all this can be resolved without anyone going to jail."

"Oh dear me, yes!" Mathers said in an extremely startled manner. "We certainly do want to avoid that. I assure you I don't consider it very likely. We may well have to pay some fines here and there. I believe a number of laws have been broken. The most important of which was leaving the scene of the crime in Nairobi. But I suppose the police will understand that a young woman without a visa might well be terrified to do so."

Melissa looked over the document he gave her, signed it, and returned it to him.

"Now, for the time being, I want you to remain here. I will phone your uncle's counsel in Nairobi and assure him that you are safe and tell him why you left Nairobi. He will take that information to the police in Kenya. They will want to see you, of course.

"In the meantime, I shall see the immigration authorities here and see what I can do. I'm on rather good terms with some highly placed members of the government and perhaps they can assist me in legalizing your presence here. That will make it possible to fly to Kenya where we will talk to your uncle's counsel and find out just what is involved in the estate and try to get you at least part of your inheritance at the earliest date feasible. Now, if you will excuse me, I must be on my way. It was a pleasure to meet you, Miss Lopes, Mrs. Richards." They both accompanied him to the door.

"I shall keep in close touch. Perhaps I will even re-turn later today, depending on what I have learned."

"Thank you, I feel much better for your visit." Me-lissa assured him truthfully.

She closed the door and Fiona chortled, "Tonio did well in finding that one."

A bit earlier than usual, Richards returned from work doing the stairs two at a time. Not easy for a man with short legs. The exertion of climbing rap-idly to the fourth floor had him puffing and red in the face. He threw his arms dramatically around his wife's neck and pretended to allow her to drag him into the flat.

"I'm lucky to have some free time today and I don't want to waste it climbing stairs," he explained, gasp-ing for air. "After I catch my breath and have a cold beer, let's drive out to Kurasini and look at the car I was telling you about. Sorry I can't ask you along for the ride, Melissa, but Tonio was in my office just be-fore I left and said he sends his love, things are going fine, and to keep you here under wraps for a day or two. He'll be here a bit later I expect."

Fiona went to the window and called down to Kathy to ask if she wanted to go for a ride.

"No, thank you. I am well suited right here," an-swered the little girl with great dignity from where she was making mud pies with her friends.

"We won't be late, Melissa. Kathy will be up soon for her supper, keep her in after that. She can do with a bathe and then bed."

"If you wish I will prepare something for your supper, too, something that can be kept hot in the oven, shall I?"

"That would be very nice. I'll be sure to pick up some magazines for you while I'm out. We are off then, take care."

It was nice to have a kitchen to herself to make a casserole for the Richards. Wonderful to have some worthwhile work to do.

Suddenly from outside came the sounds of Kathy's screams, "Don't touch it!! Nyoka! Nyoka!" *(snake)* Melissa didn't so much as close the door after herself but ran downstairs as fast as she could, wishing she had on a dress instead of a sari. She kicked off her sandals as she ran, they were threatening to trip her. She raced past other people who were coming out of their flats, too. She sped by an early arriving night watchman who had his panga in his hand as he yelled, "Nyoka! Nyoka!" while running to where the children were.

Melissa grabbed up Kathy saying, "Did it bite you? Did it bite you?"

The terrified child was wailing now and shaking with fright. Finally she stammered, "I don't know."

By now the whole area was full of Africans, Asians and a few Europeans. The askari had chopped the mamba to bits with his panga.

"Did the little girl get bitten?" Yelled one of the men.

"I don't know, but the snake bit me on the foot!" answered Melissa despairingly.

She looked around to see if there was someone there with a car that could take them to the Aga Khan hospital immediately.

An Englishwoman groaned, "Oh, if only Ian were here. I haven't a car. I'll run down to the other block of flats and see if I can borrow one. Now, not to worry." She called rather pointlessly and she ran off as fast as a woman her age and size could run. Melissa felt panic. The pain in her foot was spreading upward. The askari had found another mamba and had killed it too, much to the glee of some very young African children who didn't realize that she, and possibly Kathy also were in grave danger.

Melissa looked toward the farther block of flats the English woman had darted into, and as she turned back, she realized she was staring into the eyes of Bruno Benavides.

She felt sick in her stomach and carefully set the little girl down saying, "Kathy, I think I am going to faint." She half crumpled to the ground, put her head on her knees and tried to control the waves of nausea that were breaking over her. Benavides would just have to wait.

The English woman drove up with the door of a Volkswagen open. Bruno didn't wait for anything. He told the woman to get in the back with Kathy, he scooped up Melissa, put her in the front with him and got behind the wheel. He threw the car into reverse and started to drive like life depended on it, and of course it did.

"Our flat is unlocked," Melissa gasped and the

woman in the back called an order to the askari who answered, "Ndiyo, Mama, Ndiyo." *(Yes, Lady, Yes.)*

"He'll take care of it. Now just lie back and we'll be with a doctor soon."

They were already two blocks down the road. Benavides didn't say a word. He just concentrated on his driving which fortunately was amazingly skillful, if frightening. Melissa was vaguely aware of several motorists yelling and honking at them as he darted through traffic.

She wondered if it was the snake venom and shock or Bruno that was making her so sick. She said, "Oh, it hurts." Her lips were turning blue.

He maneuvered the car as close to the hospital entrance as he could, shut off the motor, tossed the keys to the woman in the back seat and ordered, "Park the car, please."

He got out, picked up Melissa and said to Kathy, "You come with us, be sure to stay right with us." He set off for the door calling as he ran, "Nyoka."

Nothing gets people's attention better in East Africa than the call of 'Snake!' It brought a doctor out of a room where he had been attending a patient. He commanded, "Follow me."

He lead the way into an examination room where Bruno put Melissa down on the examination table and explained that she had been bitten in the foot and that there was a possibility that the little girl had been bitten also, but that he doubted it. Another doctor appeared in the doorway and picked up Kathy to look her over for snake bites.

A hypodermic was prepared as the doctor told Benavides to wait in the reception room. He would be called later. The doctor loosened Melissa's sari and pulled her sari slip loose at the waist in order to get at the large muscle in her hip. She was aware that she was going to have the shot and felt so relieved that she didn't fell pain when the needle pierced her skin. The doctor cleansed the area with alcohol and was working on the place where the snake's fangs had entered her foot. The she felt herself slipping, sliding into a whirlpool.

"Sister, get someone to help you get her into bed, keep a close watch on her – her heartbeat is very weak."

"How is the little girl, doctor?" he called out to a colleague a few minutes later.

"Oh, she will keep. Nothing wrong with her that soap and water wouldn't cure. But she has had a bad scare. The snake must have slid past her hand and when she drew it back quickly, she scratched it on a twig, or piece of glass, and she didn't know if the snake had bitten her or not. I looked her over very carefully, and she is fine, but for the shock."

"Good. Well, come with me, little one."

Kathy was helped off the examination table and dutifully followed the doctor into the waiting room where Bruno was sitting on a window ledge smoking a cigarette.

"Are you the young woman's husband, or brother?" The doctor asked.

"No. I brought her in, together with this lady here."

and he indicated the rather stout English woman seated nearby.

"Will she recover, doctor?" the woman asked anxiously.

"I think so, barring complications."

"If you will please register the patient now, this little girl is fine, she just had a scare. She can profit by a nice cup of cocoa, a warm bath and a bedtime story, I should think."

"I am sorry, doctor, but I don't know who the other girl is. I can't remember ever seeing her before. I know the little girl, Kathy Richards, right?"

Kathy nodded mutely.

"I know the girl's name," Benavides said, and at the same time he got up and walked towards the reception desk where he quietly told the clerk that Melissa's name was Rosa Benavides, his cousin.

Bruno, the English woman, and a much confused Kathy left the hospital after the doctor told them they could come back in the morning to see how the patient was.

Melissa was put to bed and a young nurse was stationed at her bedside to keep a close watch on her pulse and breathing.

'The doctor must think I am going to live,' she thought. 'Otherwise there would be a lot more commotion.' This reassured her but at the same time she was horribly nauseated and when she noticed a bucket by the side of her bed, she leaned over it and lost what remained of her lunch. This helped somewhat, but her head ached almost as much as her foot did.

"Oh, I don't feel well." she said weakly.

"No, I don't suppose you do," the nurse agreed, "But you will be well in a few days. You were lucky you were able to get here so fast. Your cousin was clever, too. The English woman said he ran carrying you, which was good because if you'd walked, that would help spread the poison. He said it was a mamba. A terrible, terrible snake. Hospitals are the best place to be if you've been bitten—if a person has any choice in the matter...usually there is no hospital near..."

"I am so glad my little friend is all right. When she cried out, I believed she had been bitten and I was thinking of her and didn't stop to consider that the snake wouldn't be far away. There must have been a nest of them because the askari killed the one that bit me and another one, which I think was larger. The one that bit me was greenish, the other was very dark. I think it was black."

"You were probably bitten by a brown mamba, they are green when they are young. If you say the other snake was very dark, then it was probably the parent of your snake and yours was too young to be dark brown. Lucky, too, because it probably would have had more poison in it."

"You're right. But I don't like you calling the snake that bit me, my snake."

"I can see you are feeling better already!" The nurse took out her thermometer, shook it vigorously, and placed it under Melissa's tongue. "Now keep that in there for a few minutes while I take your pulse and blood pressure for the chart. Your skin isn't so pale and your pulse is stronger."

The nurse bustled around tending to Melissa, changing the compress on her wound and making her more comfortable. The area around the bite still hurt but not as much as before.

The doctor came in to see her, and then the nurse helped her into a coarse hospital gown, sponged her face and hands and she fell asleep. The pain and shock had tired her. Still, it wasn't possible to sleep for very long periods because of the pain in her foot. She was given juice and buttered bread and found that food seemed to make her feel more comfortable so she slept again.

"Good morning, Miss Benavides! I hear you had a tolerable night and are progressing well."

Benavides! Melissa thought. But aloud she said, "Thank you doctor for saving my life! I am very glad you were here."

"I had a good bit of help. Antivenin, a hypodermic to stimulate your heart and something to deaden your pain, antiseptic to clean the wound...not to mention the quick thinking of your cousin. He's in the waiting room now. He would like to see, you. I will send him in, if that's all right with you."

She couldn't very well refuse to see her 'cousin,' nor deny that her name was Benavides either, so she said simply, "Oh yes, send him in."

Bruno came in carrying a bouquet of flowers , the kind that boys sell in the market, bound together tightly with vines or stems. He put them on her night table.

Melissa looked at Bruno and thought, 'Well, this is what I was afraid of. Getting caught by him or the police, and now this happened, I don't seem to worry so. Nothing like snake bite to put things in perspective.' Aloud she smiled and said, "Very good of you to come and so kind of you to bring flowers!"

"I was anxious to see how you are."

It was all Melissa could do not to reply cynically, 'I'm sure you were.' But she said pleasantly, "I am much better and I know I have you to thank for getting me here so fast yesterday."

"I was glad I could be of service," he said formally.

"Strange that you should have been there. Do you have friends over in those flats?"

"I just arrived. I was parking my piki piki when the little girl screamed and you came running out. I intended to come up to see you."

"Blackmail?" she blurted out before she had a chance to think better of it.

"No. That was a very bad idea – which I hope we can forget."

He looked genuinely distressed, stared at the floor and said, "I read the papers so I guessed that you must be back in Dar. I followed Tonio when he went to the solicitor's office. When Tonio left there and went out the Pugu Road, I telephoned a friend of mine at the airport and he told me later that Tonio only talked to Richards while he was there.

"Everyone knows Richards because of the daily news about the rally. It all fit together, Richards had been in Nairobi, and returned. Tonio talked to him.

I just got back on my piki piki and drove over to see you. I wanted to tell you that I was very sorry for what I did and sorry too about those murders in Nairobi. I do not want to add to your problems."

"Why didn't you tell Tonio?"

"He would never believe me. Nothing will change his feelings about me. But you probably know that our families were once good friends. There was later bad feelings after a tragic mistake. It was just by chance I was able to do you a good turn. Now I hope we can be friends?" He extended his hand. Melissa was touched by his frankness and took his hand gladly. "I will be happy to have a new friend. Heaven knows I can use a few."

"By the way, if the hospital wants some proof of who you are, here is my sister's library card. If that isn't enough, let me know and I will bring her birth certificate."

"You make me feel like a weight has been lifted from my shoulders."

"The least I can do after the trouble I caused you before. I must go. I think I may find work with the Mwananchi Construction Company. I have an appointment there this morning."

"Good luck to you and I hope you find what you are looking for."

The nurse came in again, fluffed the pillows and gave her some medicine. "Your cousin is such a polite and thoughtful young man," she said dreamily.

"Hmm. He brought me some flowers, do you suppose you could find a jar of water for them?"

"Certainly."

The nurse left and Melissa pondered the changes in Bruno. *'Perhaps he has had a religious experience that changed him? No. I don't think so. Well perhaps he just felt sorry for a girl who is having problems? Perhaps. But I was just as illegal two weeks ago. It must be that after helping me, he discovered he liked being a hero better than being the villain and he changed roles. Well, no. He said he had the change of heart and was coming to tell me so when I was bitten, and I seem to believe him.'*

The nurse returned with the flowers nicely arranged in a vase and Tonio right behind her.

"You have another visitor," she purred, evidently enjoying what she probably hoped would be a parade of healthy, single young men.

Melissa motioned for Tonio to sit down on the side of her bed.

"It won't hurt you?"

"Oh no, I'm quite well now. I must stay here for a day or two, but I have had breakfast and I'm not nauseated anymore."

"Ah Melissa, I'm so glad you're all right." He sighed deeply. "When the Richards came home, Kathy was there with the English lady, and she told them what happened. Fiona drove right out to see you, but the doctor said to come back today since you were in a lot of pain, nauseated and not up to company. She drove over to my place and told me, and I came in as soon as I could this morning."

"I have been thinking about how lucky I was. I know

it would have been better not to have been bitten, but since I was, I couldn't have been more fortunate in the circumstances."

"Yes, you were even lucky that Bruno was lurking about trying to blackmail you."

"He came to see me this morning and he says he came to the flats yesterday to apologize...that he didn't want to do that anymore. He was parking his piki piki when I came running down as Kathy screamed. I know I fainted and I don't remember much of what happened for a while. He says he had a change of heart."

"No doubt. Now instead of a little money blackmailing us, he hopes to get a lot of money by being the rescuer of an heiress. The snake unexpectedly helped him out."

"Tonio, he even registered me as his cousin and he does seem remorseful."

"Really, Melissa—when he went to see you, it was because of the newspaper story about you being the only heir of your rich uncle. When you were bitten, it was an opportunity for him to get in your good graces and he is clever enough to seize any opportunity that comes his way."

"Don't you think he would have helped if I were someone he didn't know?"

"He probably would have, if it didn't cost him much, and there was something to be gained. Granted, I am grateful he was there when he was."

"Tonio, you are cynical!"

"No. I just believe that smiles and talk of turning

over a new leaf, and I suppose – flowers – those are his flowers...?"

"Yes."

"I want to see a bit more of this new page he's turning over before I decide that he is a friend. Still, it's nice not to worry about him anymore."

"I liked the solicitor you sent," Melissa said abruptly.

"I thought you would. He has an excellent reputation and knows just what steps we should take. I didn't want him to know where you were, in case the police or the press ask him questions. I didn't know exactly where to take you. Now that problem has been solved, at least for a day or two, 'Miss Benavides' my love."

"'It's an ill wind that blows no good,' or something like that." said Melissa with a weary shrug.

"Must get back to work. I'll be here late this afternoon and bring you the papers and some magazines. Do you want anything else?'

"Well, if it isn't too much trouble, you could stop in at Hatimi's and buy me some butterscotch drops."

"I'll get some." He bent and kissed her and whispered in her ear.

"I love you, too." she said in a soft voice.

CHAPTER EIGHT

"Well, I've always heard that an easy conscience is the best pillow, but I didn't realize that it worked that way at mid-day." Fiona was fondly stroking Melissa's forehead as she spoke softly to her.

"Good morning Fiona. Have you been here long?" Melissa asked drowsily.

"No. I just arrived. I took Kathy to her nursery school and I've been various places trying to buy milk. I can't thank you enough for rushing down to care for our little girl. I know you simply did what came naturally to you. You could not have done otherwise, no matter what. We certainly have been worried about you!"

"I'm fine now, thank you. I myself was good and worried for a bit. By the way, Fiona, Benavides was here this morning too, and he said that he came over last night to tell me he's changed and is sorry for his attempt at blackmail. He wants to be my friend."

"Good grief, that's all you need! How did he know where to find you?"

"He saw Tonio talking to your husband, put two facts together. Your family was recently in Nairobi and the newspapers told where I was. He'd just arrived when I came tearing down the stairs after Kathy screamed."

"Mrs. Waters, the English lady who was such a help, was taking care of Kathy in her flat when we returned. There was a note on our door telling us the number of her flat. She told us you are a cousin of the man who drove you to the Aga Khan hospital.

"I said I didn't know about that, but that it wouldn't surprise me because you know how some Goan families are, related to all others in East Africa. It isn't remotely true, but it seemed to satisfy her natural curiosity. She seems a good sort."

"Yes. She didn't take the attitude that because she had no car she couldn't be expected to help. She just ran off and borrowed one. Very English of her."

Fiona brought the papers and some of her Women's Magazines and that entertained Melissa for a while. She didn't want to think much about being returned to Zanzibar nor about being tried for crimes in Nairobi.

When Tonio came to see her, she said, "The doctor told me I can leave here tomorrow noon. I will be glad, of course, but where should I go?"

"Mrs. Gomes is anxious to have you return to stay with her, she says she needs the company. I'll collect you here after work tomorrow noon and take you to her. I know the Richards will understand."

"Something that troubles me, Tonio, is what do I do about the hospital bill? I suppose I will have some money some day, but I surely don't now."

"Not to worry. I have money for that. The important news is that Mathers is flying to Nairobi tonight, he has appointments with your uncle's solicitor and with the Nairobi Police. He told me to tell you that he's sure there will be no 'insurmountable problems' to use his exact words."

"You know, Tonio, sometimes I think..." her voice trailed off as she tried to find a way to put her thoughts into words that might convince Tonio.

"No need to explain. We all think, from time to time." he said teasingly.

"No, Tonio, be serious. I wanted to say that I think perhaps you and I should take on that business and become merchants." She looked up at him quizzically.

Tonio took some time before he replied, "I gave it a good bit of thought myself. But I decided against it. Your uncle and his son ran the business alone. The other workers were just doing as they were told. We wouldn't know what to do, there is no one to tell us and in no time at all we would have lost more money than you inherited."

"Perhaps we could hire someone knowledgeable in the trade?"

"Who would that be? Most of the Asian and English merchants have already left the country. You yourself told me that your uncle had an emergency plan for leaving in the event that there was another movement against Asians. No, Kenya may be tolerating a few Asians and a handful of English nationals, but it is just until Africans can take over without swamping the economy...perhaps it would help a bit if we were citizens of Kenya. But we aren't."

"It is wrong of them to force businessmen out of the country they have lived in so long." Melissa said rebelliously.

"Kenya wants to be independent. And she wants

her businesses to be run by Kenyans. I can understand that."

"Yes, but many of those that had to leave were Kenyan citizens and their families were too."

"That's true. All resident foreigners had a choice at Independence – to retain their British passports or throw in their lot with the newly independent country. Not many of them chose Kenyan citizenship, and naturally, the Kenyans don't feel particularly obligated to them even though they were born in the country."

"Why didn't they take Kenyan citizenship? I'm sure I would have."

"Yes. I would have, too. But think of it from the point of view of people who have a long history of not being wanted anywhere. British citizenship is a wonderful thing. It gives you rights, advantages, protection of English law and that is not something Asians wanted to give up. The majority of them wish Kenya great success and always intended to live there. But they also knew there was a great deal of anti-Asian feeling and that many black Africans believe that only when all Europeans and Asians have gone will the black Africans really come into their own."

"But how can they expect to know how to run businesses, hospitals, schools or even how to fix the plumbing?"

"Those with education know that they can't do those things alone at this stage of development. But the pressure from the uneducated hot heads to take over property is great. Kenya is, after all, a place where people get elected to public office. How can anyone get elected by saying they intend to protect the rights of foreigners? Much easier if you say you will kick them out and divide the profits among the black Africans."

"Yes. I guess I really knew that. And you just don't think we could run that business either."

"I know we couldn't. Selling it now, you will at least get something for it."

"We will get something for it." She corrected him, "Not just me."

"I feel rather strange about that. I always loved you when you were homeless, penniless and wanted by the police 'to help their enquiries.' But I haven't had time to adjust to being in love with an heiress." He spoke with an attempt at humor but his voice betrayed concern.

"You will just have to learn to take the sweet with the bitter. You have had plenty of time to share my woes, it will be great to have you join me in good fortune."

"Perhaps there won't be much left after death duties, solicitors' expenses and we don't actually know what condition your uncle's business was in. Maybe there are zillions of creditors."

"I wonder if you half hope that there will be."

"No. Not really. It probably won't be hard to adjust to having money. Setting up housekeeping is said to be expensive. Oh yes, I almost forgot, but speaking of expenses, here are your butterscotch drops and some others."

At noon the next day, Tonio arrived to take her to Mrs. Gomes' apartment. She felt very weak and tired by the time she'd climbed the stairs. Tonio went back to work. Mrs. Gomes propped Melissa up in bed and served her hot tea and samosas while Melissa told her the details that weren't in the paper about her stay in Nairobi. Mrs. Gomes knew the general outlines from the newspapers, but it was especially horrifying to have her dear little friend tell the parts that weren't in the paper. It made danger feel too near.

After commending her and her dead family to the care of our Lord and letting her own tears fall down her face, she made an effort to be cheerful. "My daughter writes often asking for a photo of the two of us. I have been sending her the most interesting letters recently and some quite shocking ones, as you can well imagine. She wants to see what you look like. I would like to take you over to a photographer's shop only a block from here and have some pictures made tomorrow. I think you will be feeling even stronger by then and Melendes, the photographer, is an old friend of our family."

"Is it safe for me to have photos taken?"

"Yes, I'll just tell him not to put them in the window."

The next morning, Melissa and Mrs. Gomes dressed carefully, fussed over their hair and tried on one necklace after another until they finally decided they looked their best. Melissa felt stronger, but she still walked slowly.

The photographer's shop was antiquated compared

to the modern shops of Nairobi, but not unlike those she knew in Zanzibar. In the window there were a couple of photos of Goan children on the occasion of their first communion, an African couple in wedding attire and two photos of African army officers.

Mr. Melendes greeted them warmly and said he would begin at once with a pose of the two of them. He seated them before a backdrop which looked like Tarzan's jungle. He moved an arm one way, the chin of the other until he had them posed to his satisfaction in what Melissa realized would look like two well dressed ladies stranded in the Congo. It made her smile, which pleased him and he clicked the shutter. "Just so!" He took two more poses of them together and then announced, "Now for the individual poses." He rubbed his hands together and looked thoughtful for a moment and then began to move his scenery about so that he had Mrs. Gomes seated in front of what looked to be a cross between Mount Fujiyama and Kilimanjaro.

The front door was pushed open, the bell on it tinkled insistently and a loud voice demanded, "Where are you, old man? We need work done. Get out here!"

Mr. Melendes' face lost its pleasant smile and his voice shook as he said, "Excuse me, ladies...they...we, they..." and he left the little room to attend to the noisy and rude soldiers. There were no less than half a dozen of them by the sound of it.

"Take my picture, old man, and be quick!"

"Where is your donation for the officers' fund?"

Each had a demand, no one waited for an answer.

Melissa got up quietly and peeked out the side of the curtain. "There are six Africans in uniform out there...one of them has just shoved Melendes!"

"Let's go!" said Mrs. Gomes who was visibly alarmed.

"How? Is there a back entrance?"

"No, there isn't. But this room connects to the dark-room. We can wait in there while he takes pictures of the Africans."

When the noise in the other room was even louder, Melissa turned the knob on the door leading into the darkroom and the two women slipped into it and made themselves as comfortable as they could on the floor. One of the soldiers had announced he would be the first to be photographed and he elbowed his way past Melendes who was trying to dissuade him.

The African burst into the room and Melendes hurried in behind him and knew with relief where his former customers must be. He said in a loud voice, "I will have your photos made immediately, but the rest of you will have to return after the midday meal. I am expecting film in the mail and I cannot do justice to more than one with what I have on hand."

There were sounds of disgust, but no one seemed to question the truthfulness of the statement and so he went about the business of taking the most professional pictures he could of the haughty soldier.

"There. I have taken four nice poses. We should have some good results from these. You can come back tomorrow and choose, if you would like."

"Yes. I will be here tomorrow. Have a good contribution ready for me then, too." And with that order, he left.

Mr. Melendes opened the darkroom door and light flooded in as they got to their feet and their eyes adjusted. "I have nothing drying in here now – I am so sorry about the intrusion. This is becoming very common. It would be bad enough having to do so much work free of charge, but I am constantly harassed for contributions. If I don't give them, there are threats. I have made up my mind to leave the country."

"Where will you go?" Mrs. Gomes asked anxiously.

"I have an Indian passport," he answered in a sad, tired voice while he stared down at the floor.

"India!" His old friend said with what sounded like shock in her voice.

"I know what you are thinking; so crowded, so poor, and I don't know anyone there anymore. But I can't stay here. Most of the soldiers and policemen who come in for pictures are polite and willing to pay. But there isn't so much profit in the business that I can afford to have several of them demand free work every day – not to mention more money demanded in contributions than I take in. None of them have ever been in business and they just seem to believe that I have only to open the shop door in order to make large profits!"

"Isn't there anywhere else you could go?" Melissa asked.

"I don't think so. The world looks so large when you look at a map. You would think there would be somewhere for a man like me. No matter. Come back tomorrow and let's finish up the work."

They walked slowly back to the apartment. "It's so very, very, very unfair." Melissa protested.

"Yes." Her friend said simply.

Kenyatta Avenue in downtown Nairobi, Kenya.
(Circa 1969)

CHAPTER NINE

Melissa was scarcely awake in the morning when Mrs. Gomes knocked on the door to say, "Sorry to disturb you, there is a messenger here from Mr. Mathers' office and he has a note for you." She handed it to Melissa who brushed her hair out of her eyes and sat up in bed as she extended a rather shaky hand for the note.

"I don't think it is anything to worry about, dear."

It wasn't or didn't seem to be. "No, he just asks if I can come to his office to discuss plans this morning at ten." She sighed with relief.

"The messenger is still here. You write something on the note and I'll have him take it back to Mathers."

Melissa wrote on the bottom of the note that she would be in at ten.

"What time is it now, then?" She asked when Mrs. Gomes came back from seeing the messenger out.

"Only nine. His office is about ten minutes from here, even if you walk slowly. I'll prepare coffee, toast and some sliced fruit while you shower and dress."

$\sim\!\!\mathcal{M}\!\!\sim$

"Good morning, Melissa. Right on time." Mathers obviously approved of people being exactly on time. He looked at the wall clock and then checked his pocket watch and made sure that they both said ten o'clock exactly. "I think we ought to fly to Nairobi soon. In fact, the sooner the better. We have a buyer for the house and we should strike while the iron is hot. Also, I have been informed by this morning's post that your uncle's solicitor in Nairobi believes he may have a buyer for much of the goods stored in the godown. He warns me that there will be little profit in the deal, but think we should hurry right along. When could you go?"

"I am free at any time. I would have to borrow money for the fare, however," she added ruefully.

"No, no. Not to worry. I am keeping a strict accounting of the money I spend on your behalf and rest assured, I shall collect my part. I have my obligations you know – and this is purely a business transaction."

"Well, that's good. How long do you suppose we will be gone?"

"I think that it will take us three days. It could all be done in one afternoon, but experience has taught me that would be extremely unlikely. Someone won't be there, or a proper stamp will be needed. Yes, I would plan on three days."

"Thank you, Mr. Mathers, I will go home and pack and be waiting. What time?"

"Six thirty this evening in front of the Gomes flat. See you then." He courteously arose and walked her to the outer office door.

Mathers returned to his desk and sat there for a moment pondering the inequities of fate and talking aloud to himself, "She said she would go 'home' and pack, she meant Gomes', of course. I can't see how she can live in East Africa." He cleared his throat and picked up another file, another problem but a bit easier to solve.

Because Nairobi is so much cooler than Dar, she packed a sweater and a light jacket and decided to take stockings too, an item rarely worn in Dar or Zanzibar, but it might look peculiar to be barelegged in the business offices of Nairobi. She wasn't a Zanzibari girl going to Nairobi on holiday, she was now the only heir of a wonderful family. She wanted to be what would be expected.

A knock on the door interrupted her private conversation with herself, "Melissa, are you there?"

"I'm coming, Mrs. Gomes." she called as she ran to open the door.

"I have the key in here somewhere but I am too tired and miserable to go through this purse if I don't have to. Oh, my poor jaw!" She put down her over-sized purse and sat her plump self down, while one hand supported her aching jaw.

"Did the dentist pull the tooth?"

"No, but I think he did everything else. I know it will be fine in an hour or so, right now..."

"Come out and have a cup of tea, you won't even have to chew a little fruit salad I made. It's all soft fruits. You'll feel better with a bit of tea and food." Mrs. Gomes who usually gave the orders and helped other people, followed Melissa meekly into the tiny kitchen and did as she was told. This amused Melissa so much that she had a hard time keeping a straight face.

"I am going to Nairobi with Mr. Mathers this afternoon. He's coming for me here at 6:30; we expect to be gone three days."

"Well, I wish you the best of luck. Take anything you need. I'll be expecting you back in three days time, but you have a key, so you can always just come in."

"I wish I didn't have to go," Melissa blurted out.

"Anyone would understand that! Where will you be staying?"

"Mr. Mathers said that we would be at the Ngong Hotel."

"You'll enjoy it. You weren't there the last time, were you?"

"No, the Richards stay at the New Stanley. The Ngong is very grand and new, not quite finished."

"Enjoy the elegant new hotel, Melissa. No good can come of letting yourself feel frightened and miserable and your uncle certainly wouldn't want that."

"I wish they'd caught the murderers." Melissa exclaimed vehemently.

"Are you afraid for yourself?" Mrs. Gomes asked with genuine concern showing in her face.

"No – no, I don't think I had anything to do with that. They didn't really expect to find me there, they would have broken into the bathroom and killed me if they knew I was there."

"Yes, but now that they do know you were there, they may think you could point them out, have you thought of that?"

"I thought about it, but they know I have been in touch with the police; it has been in all the papers and on radio. Surely they must know that I would have pointed out the murderers by now if I could. I don't think they could possibly believe I am a threat."

"I'm sure you are right. It's just that you would like to know that justice has been done."

"Yes, I am not particularly vindictive, or at least I don't think I am. I learned not to be when my father's killers went free."

"No. they didn't really go free. There is punishment for crime even in this world— fear of being found out, remorse— there is always something, even if we don't recognize it. And if they escape in this world, God will take care of it in the next."

Mrs. Gomes turned on the radio and they listened to BBC to get their minds off Melissa's problem. The announcer spoke of the tide of Asians coming into English cities, of changing neighborhoods and that the English were distressed to see this happen.

"I can understand their concern, Mrs. Gomes, but what are all the East African Asians supposed to do? No one thought much about it when a tyrant on a tiny island in the Indian Ocean decided to take the property of Arabs and Asians. No one did a thing to stop it. The UN was unconcerned, the U.S. sent them more foreign aid, Asian women were forced into marriage. President Nyerere of Tanzania flew to Zanzibar to help one particular group of women. But no one else helped. It was 'deplored' on the back pages of world newspapers. Now many people are trying to get into the UK where they are legally entitled to be. They often don't truly want to live there, but they must. Who can blame the English for not turning their little island into a gigantic refugee camp? Still, a place to live doesn't seem too much to ask."

Fortunately, Tonio arrived then and sat with Melissa on the veranda. She told him of her plans to go to Nairobi and he seemed relieved she was going to get it over with.

"I'll miss you, but the trip will tie up loose ends, the things that you can do, you will be able to do. Then I think you and I will feel happier all around."

"Yes. I know you're right."

"I'll drive you to the airport."

"No need. Mr. Mathers' driver will take us out. If you don't mind, you can come and collect us on Thursday, though. I'll try and get word to you if we can't come in on the Thursday evening plane from Nairobi. Sometimes the phones work just fine."

Tonio suggested that he and Melissa nip over to a nearby restaurant and buy samosas and Coca Cola. They ran off like school children and brought back the hot spicy little pies, fresh from the boiling oil. Melissa was about to reach for her fourth when Mrs. Gomes said, "Oh dear, I wonder if samosas are recommended food for air travelers."

"I doubt it." Tonio said. "Better not have any more of them and drink some Coca Cola. Someone once told me Cola is good at settling the stomach."

At 6:30 on the dot, the three of them were standing

with Melissa's suitcase in front of the building when Mr. Mathers arrived. "Good! Punctuality, that's the ticket!"

After hurried goodbyes, the chauffeur drove them off in the shiny black Mercedes Benz.

The multi-colored East African Airlines plane was waiting and ready for boarding as they checked their luggage and settled down in their seats.

A pretty African stewardess told them she would have supper for them soon.

Melissa giggled thinking of her samosas and how that was now to be followed by another meal. Still, when the beautifully arranged tray came, it looked good and she enjoyed it. "I shall be fat as a pig." She said aloud.

Mathers asked, "What, what?" He wasn't used to her habit of talking aloud to herself from time to time.

"Nothing." She smiled, and he went back to his reading. Melissa thought it was no wonder that there were so few fat Englishmen because they can read the paper and eat without giving a moment's thought to the food. She remembered Fiona and her ability to drink the blood and milk in the Masai Boma. Many English women are good cooks, but they didn't ever let on that they actually take eating very seriously, just something one does.

She just finished her coffee as they prepared to land. They were met at the airport by Mr. Montero, her uncle's solicitor, and swiftly conveyed by yet another black Mercedes Benz to the superbly modern Ngong Hotel.

So far, Melissa hadn't had a moment to feel afraid, or even sad. She had a sharp twinge as they drove down a street that she had driven down not long ago with her uncle, but she purposely pushed back any dark feeling of horror that threatened to blacken her mood and listened instead to the small talk of the two men in the front seat of the sedan.

They told her they would make plans that evening and that she should simply get a good night's sleep and leave things to them.

Her room overlooked a great sweep of Nairobi with the Ngong Ngong Hills in the background. Once again, she marveled at the beauty of this modern city set in the middle of a primitive land. She bathed, read some brochures that had been left in the room and fell asleep easily.

She woke very early and rather wished she hadn't. Mathers would call. Therefore, due to a law she believed must be in force, if she left long enough to buy a newspaper or to get a cup of coffee, he would surely phone and find her gone. So she entertained herself by writing a letter to Tonio on hotel stationery. She was idly turning the radio dial when the phone finally rang and Mathers said she should meet him downstairs in the coffee shop for a good breakfast.

She applied just a bit of eye shadow, surveyed herself in the mirror and decided she looked fine and that no one would ever suspect that the well cut beige silk suit she was wearing belonged to someone else.

Breakfast, she realized, was going to be one of those large English affairs. The waiter was at the table when she arrived and Mathers was looking at the menu. "Have a nice kipper, my dear. Nothing like it to sustain one."

"Thank you, but I believe I shall just have juice, a roll, and coffee."

When his kipper arrived, he tucked into it without any real enthusiasm, but with what was probably his belief that it would do him a world of good.

"Your first appointment is with the police. I have an old friend in the department who will sit in on the meeting as a courtesy to us. Might get a bit sticky, you understand."

"Why?" she asked with alarm.

"One never knows. The older fellows will be fine, but there is usually some young chap looking for quick promotion who will be a bit over-bearing. Insist on the letter, rather than the spirit of the law...that sort of thing, don't you know."

Melissa didn't, but she could easily imagine such a scenario.

The Police commissioner's office was plain, but comfortable and he treated them with courtesy and understanding. "Please be seated, my secretary will come in to take notes of our meeting. I understand John Bradley is a friend of yours and he will sit in on the meeting too."

The questioning was very matter of fact and Melissa was asked if she could remember any of the faces.

"No. I can't. I didn't see any of them."

"Can you remember the voices?"

"No. I can't." She had thought so many times that

there was some small thing that should remind her of something, but it had never crystallized in her mind, so she had nothing to tell.

"Any detail, no matter how insignificant it may be to you, could be the key to solving this crime, so if anything ever occurs to you, do not hesitate to contact us. Anything, anytime."

"Yes, sir certainly. And thank you."

"We have not closed the books on this matter and we won't either. It is very possible that the crime may not be solved for years, but there were just too many people involved for it to remain a mystery forever. One of them will be drinking and tell all, or the men will have a squabble amongst themselves, one of them will get clear and then turn the rest in by mail. Any notion that there is honor among thieves and murderers is just so much poppycock!"

"My client would like to sign the papers you have ready for her."

"Fine. In the absence of the relatives, we had to station a policeman at the scene to prevent theft, to discourage sight seers and that sort of thing. Earrings, rings and so on were put in boxes and sealed and are in the vault over here. This was done with the solicitor of your late uncle present."

"That was very thoughtful of you."

"Routine. I think some of the jewels are probably almost worthless and some of the carpets on the floor are what should really be here in the vault!" They smiled at each other, both thinking of the collection of plastic earrings that had belonged to her cousins and were now reposing with a few good things in the police vault.

Mathers looked at the papers that were ready for Melissa's signature and indicated with a nod to her they they should be signed.

The Commissioner accepted the papers and asked, "Where did you go after you left your uncle's house?"

Melissa felt reluctant to involve the Richards, so she had a short conversation with Mr. Mathers before answering. He advised her to tell them since it would be plain to see why she hadn't wished to remain in the country and easy to understand that the Richards would take her back with them.

The Commissioner was annoyed. "How can anyone expect us to do our work properly after a crime when people merely go about their ordinary business! Would it be too much to let us know when murders are committed?"

"I am sorry, Sir. But I didn't go to the Richards right away. I was so terrified, I was afraid of everything at that time. I am Zanzibari and I have lived through some horrors, my own father was killed in front of me. I suppose that is beside the point." she shuddered. "When I left the house, I went to the Pan Afrique Hotel, hoping to take a taxi to the airport and perhaps go to Mombasa and from there escape again by sea—to where, I really didn't know. Not being a citizen, I was sure I would be held by the police, if not for murders, then at least for illegal entry into the country.

"By the time I saw Richards it was very late. Just a few hours before time for the servants to begin the morning's work. I should have called you. I just couldn't. And Richards perhaps should have called, but by then, the men would certainly have been far away and in calling you, he would have put me in a very bad position."

She was panting with the effort of saying all this. For a European or American girl the effort would not have been so much, but for Melissa who had been raised to let the men do the talking, it was almost as though she had chosen to be insolent. She felt ashamed for defending herself and Richards so vehemently. She looked at the Commissioner and saw that he was amazed at her, too. His wife no doubt had proper African ladylike ways, she probably covered her mouth modestly when she laughed, and was always gentle and respectful. Just thinking about it made Melissa feel discouraged. Mr. Mathers' friend, John Bradley, smiled and nodded at her.

Mathers was beaming his full approval. He spoke up and said firmly. "Just so, just so, couldn't have put it better myself. She really does make it all very clear, doesn't she, Gentlemen?"

"Yes, it certainly is easy to understand, but I still say, we would appreciate being informed. This is not Zanzibar, after all. We are not your enemy." The Commissioner said heatedly.

Melissa looked at him and said mournfully in Swahili, "Pole sana Bwana." She wasn't sure if her, "I am very sorry, sir." was because she hadn't notified the police or because sometimes the police aren't your friends.

An assistant brought in a series of photos and Melissa was asked if any of them looked at all familiar. She knew beforehand that none of them would, but in order not to seem a "know it all" she went over each one and returned them with a shake of her head.

The Commissioner thanked her, told her he hoped matters would go well for her and acted both professional and kind. But how could she have known that on the night of the murders? "That wasn't too bad, was it?" Mathers remarked, more as a sign of satisfaction than as a question.

"No. But I was afraid for a moment when I told about going to the Richards."

"Yes, but when I saw who was at the meeting, and who wasn't, I determined it would be best to tell where you went and with whom."

"We never did tell him that the Richards knew I was here illegally."

"No, and if you noticed, they were careful not to ask!"

"I am glad you are with me. I might have said the same things without you, but I doubt it."

"Proud of you in there. You really spoke right up, delighted to hear it."

"Thank you. I felt bold and forward and I could see that the Africans thought so, too."

"Pity that. Women have to learn to speak up. Usually will when matters get to a pretty pass, often more apt to speak up for others than for themselves.

We should be on our way to Mr. Montero's office. He told us he would be in all morning and that we should stop by when we finished our police business. It isn't quite noon yet."

A taxi took them to the office and Mathers handed her out of the car with old school courtesy, which pleased her and reminded her that she wasn't really the school girl the newspapers portrayed.

Mr. Montero was also a Goan and had heard many stories about tragedies on Zanzibar, so he felt well disposed toward her. He smiled delightedly when he saw her and fished a letter out of the mess on top of his desk and hurried over to hand it to her.

"This just came this morning, from Zanzibar!" Melissa's legs felt like they were going to give way. She hadn't felt so weak since recovering from snake bite.

"This letter left Zanzibar in the care of a businessman returning to Tanzania. He, in turn, mailed it from Moshi, Tanzania to me and it has just arrived."

Melissa opened the envelope carefully and read,

Dear Melissa,

We have learned from the newspapers about your terrible troubles and wish we could be there to help you. Roberto is still working. When we read the name of the solicitor in Nairobi, we determined to get word to you through him that we are all well and hope sometime that we will be together again. A merchant friend of ours is leaving for the mainland; he will take this note.
Love Always,
Rita and Roberto

"It was just a note telling me that they are well, that they they have read about me in the papers. I feel so happy to know that no harm has come to them because of me. Roberto still has work, for instance." She carefully put it back in the envelope and then into her purse.

Mr. Montero was about to say something, but Mathers cleared his throat abruptly, "Harrumph! Well, shall we get on to the godown, or shall we stop for lunch first?" Melissa was surprised to see Montero grinning at Mathers and then realized why. Montero knew that because of Mathers' upbringing he couldn't show how moved he was by Melissa's pleasure at receiving the letter.

"Let's go to lunch first. I can explain things over the meal."

Just a few days earlier, Melissa would have felt very ill at ease listening to the conversation of her two legal advisors, but now she found herself understanding more and being interested in the talk about business and legal concerns.

During lunch, Montero said cheerfully "I have the papers for the sale of the house ready at the office and the manager of Alitalia will be in to complete the sale on behalf of his company so that should be no trouble. I will phone Mr. Bhanji, the merchant who is expected to buy the goods in the godown. Perhaps he can come along with us this afternoon. I plan to go with you since I have already looked over the books and have a fair idea of what has been paid so far from overseas suppliers. We have the invoices ready to hand so we can make some decision on what amount should be paid for the merchandise."

"I presume my client must accept a loss?" Mathers asked.

"Yes. I wish it were not so, but with so many Asians leaving and their status so unsure...This proposed buyer is an Ismaili Muslim, a citizen of Kenya since before Independence. If you remember, the Aga Khan suggested his Ismaili Muslims take citizenship where they live and Bhanji did so. He feels a bit more secure than the non citizen merchants."

"Perhaps he might pay full price then?" Melissa asked shyly, not only because it was her money, but because she thought it was an interesting business problem.

"Hardly. He has to have someone to sell to – and with so many Europeans and Asians leaving, who will have the money to buy? Most of the Africans are not in the money economy and other Africans are losing jobs and so they aren't in any position to take over the businesses. Of course, there will always be some market, but actually, Mr. Bhanji is going in very deeply to buy so much. Perhaps he hopes, or even expects, to be able to get the trade your uncle had."

The business with its now quiet office and dead seeming godown looked the same and yet the feeling was completely different. It was much like returning to a home you once lived in, finding it looks the same and yet just knowing you don't live there changes everything. This was the last piece of her family's business in East Africa. Years of work and a way of life were gone.

The merchant, Mr. Bhanji, was already parked on the tarmac near the office door.

He got out of the car to greet them and extended his sympathy to Melissa. The two solicitors, the merchant and Melissa were let into the office by the fundi who had been kept on. He seemed surprised to see Melissa again, but remembered to offer condolences with a polite, "Pole sana." She thanked him and he went off to find some extra chairs.

Melissa quietly asked Mathers, "I don't understand this well, what shall I do?"

"We are all working somewhat in the dark. We do know what is owed and what is paid for, and how much of that is on hand. Now, Mr. Bhanji will look over the books and the stock and then decide if he can take it all, or just a part of it. We will try to get 80% of its value. He won't agree to that and will offer us 50% and we will finally strike a deal somewhere in the middle. If you want to, you can go and look at the materials while we go over the first part of the deal. I know that women often enjoy looking at fabrics and if you want to take a few yards you can certainly do so."

CHAPTER TEN

As she walked through the door into the godown, she noticed what seemed like an eerie, other worldly feeling. With her cousin George, a few weeks ago, there were several fundis wheeling bolts in and out and the back doors were open to the sunshine. Now there was dim electric light, and the doors were closed. There were no windows and the air felt still, and dead.

The bolts of brightly colored, beautifully designed kanga and kitenge fabric used extensively by the Africans and always in demand, were piled high on the upper gallery. There wasn't a real second floor, just a wide walkway fifty feet above the floor of the building, with a railing all round to keep people and materials from falling to the floor below.

Downstairs at the far end of the building, there were lovely silks from India, embroidered materials from Switzerland and satins in many colors.

I think I shall have a cream colored satin for a wedding gown , she said to herself, and now two nice pieces for dressy clothes and she chose two Swiss embroideries.

She was really beginning to warm to this pleasant task and she talked quietly to herself or hummed as she examined the bolts, wishing there were a bit more light. The dim unshaded light bulbs made it hard to distinguish color tones, let alone black from navy blue.

A loud whooshing sound made her look up quickly, just in time to see a large bolt fall from the upper level. There was no time to run – she fell back and there was a deep thud, then another sound, another paper covered bolt of goods was being pushed under the railing, a whoosh and a thud and then another. She never knew whether she fainted or was knocked out by the blow on the head. When she heard the first sound and saw the bolt falling, she fell back on the materials she had set aside. This kept her from breaking her head open on the concrete floor. The handle of the trolley on which goods was moved had been hit sharply by the first falling bale, it had turned over and born the brunt of the weight of the heavy bolt as well as protecting Melissa's body from the bolts that followed.

She lay there for a moment, sheltered by the overturned trolley on one side, but visible to anyone looking down from the gallery. At first she felt too frightened to move. But that lasted for only seconds. If she stayed where she was, her attacker might think she was dead, but even so, he would be likely to come down to make sure. Her only chance lay in getting to the door of the office. Her head ached furiously and her foot did, too. The second bale had not landed on her foot or it would have smashed it, but the falling bale had pushed the handle of the trolley against it where it was still sore from the effects of the snake bite.

At any time, more bales might come crashing down on her. She forced herself to her feet and ran screaming toward the office door. The huge outer door to the godown was opened with a tremendous clang of corrugated metal which reverberated through the building. Light poured in.

Even as she ran, she heard bare feet running outside on the gravel.

The door to the office was flung open and Montero and Mathers stood looking stunned and uncomprehending. "Oh thank heaven!" Melissa exclaimed as she reached Mathers who realized that she was going to faint and gently helped her to a chair. Bhanji had noticed the huge bales on the floor, looked at the battered girl and was already turning his car around to pursue the fundi who had raced off. Montero was on the phone informing the police and Mathers was bending solicitously over Melissa.

"I'm all right." she said weakly, "He tried to kill me, he pushed the bolts over to hit me from the gallery, but the trolley fell and saved me." She gestured toward the road, "It is all clear now, he was with the men who killed my uncle and his family. I knew there was something I should have remembered and I couldn't seem to do it. I didn't even think of it when I saw him, but when I was under that trolley – I knew. I felt just like I did in the locked bathroom that night – terrified and trapped. And then I remembered that my cousin George had scolded that same fundi severely when I was here before. My cousin was harsh in his scolding, I thought. I forgot all that soon. I remember that I did hear one voice that seemed familiar to me in the house that awful night, but I only heard it once before and I didn't connect it with anyone, nor with this godown. Now I know."

"Yes, he reckoned that you would remember sooner or later. Easier, just to kill you and run away. Even if they determined it wasn't an accident he would be nowhere to be found and his friends would never be in trouble for the first crime either."

"My head aches, do you suppose there is any water here to drink? I have a couple aspirin in my purse."

"I think we will get you back to the hotel. I can come back later and finish up and you can sign the papers tonight or tomorrow. In the meantime, it might be a good idea to see a doctor."

"No, I don't need one, just some aspirin, and a cold cloth on my head."

"Hmm, yes, you do have quite a lump rising there on your forehead."

Melissa got slowly to her feet, and supported by Mathers, she got into the back seat of Montero's car. Montero said he would see to Melissa and that Mathers should stay on the scene and wait for the merchant who would probably be back soon and probably empty handed. The police would arrive in an hour or two with any luck.

"You have not had good experiences in Nairobi!" said Montero, rather more to himself than to her, as he wheeled his car around toward the city.

Melissa didn't bother to sit up because it made her head pound furiously, but she answered him with conviction, "Well, I do know one of the murderers and I suppose I know part of the reason. He was angry at an unjust scolding and who knows what else. None of it justifies what he did, but if he and the gang with him already hated Asians, that helps explain the original murders. When they found out that I was in the house that night, it probably made them think I'd better be killed, too or I might remember something and get them all in trouble. The man today was the only one I heard speaking. He was the fundi who helped me at the godown the day I was there with my cousin."

"I am afraid that we have reached a point where it is impossible to correct anyone, even in a kind way unless they are of the same color, the same class or the same nationality, preferably all three. Everyone feels sure he is being corrected because of skin color instead of because of error. No one will be corrected, no one will learn anything very complicated and all will start from the beginning as if each were another Adam." Montero had obviously said all this before.

He drove to her hotel, parked the car and insisted on helping her up the elevator and right into her own room.

"Now, just stay here. Keep the door locked and if you want anything, call room service. I will return to the godown."

"Thank you. You have been very helpful."

"Not at all, I am sorry you have had another terrible day here, but I do think it is fair to say that we are going to sell all the merchandise. Just rest now."

He left the room and told her to lock the door behind him, chain and all.

⌒⁀⌒

Melissa realized her heart was beating very rapidly and she felt more afraid now than she did before the attack in the godown. She wished she had some company. "Never mind, I'll take my aspirins and lie down with a cold cloth on my head and listen to music on the radio." She said to herself and prepared to do just that.

She pulled the draperies so that the light wouldn't be in her eyes, slipped off her shoes and jacket, took her two aspirin and crawled into bed because the air conditioning made the room cold.

She lay quietly in bed and listened to music and soon felt quite comfortable; her headache was gone and the lump on her head was only sore when she touched it.

The radio announcer surprised her by saying, "We interrupt this program to ask anyone who knows the whereabouts of Paul Mwenzaka to get in touch with the police immediately. This man is wanted in connection with the brutal killings of the Lopes family last month and for the attempted murder of their niece today. I repeat, please inform the police if you know where Paul Mwenzaka may be apprehended."

"No. They haven't found him yet. Perhaps they never will."

She wanted him and the others who were with him on that awful night to be found Feeling restless she got up and padded softly across the carpeted floor to the drapery covered window, drew the material aside and looked out on the city. The noise and chill of the air conditioner were beginning to bother her and make her head feel stuffed up. She looked around for a way to turn off the air conditioning, found the control and felt the cold air stop. She went back to the windows, unlocked them and opened them wide to let the warmer street air in. It felt wonderful.

She stood looking out at the sweep of the city before her, its sounds unmuffled by the whir of the air conditioner. She marveled at all the activity, gazed at the beauty of the white and gold mosque domes, and the Ngong Ngong hills in the distance. She felt less nervous and quite rested and decided to bathe and dress in fresh clothes, so she pulled the draperies closed again and began to unzip her skirt A discreet knock at the door interrupted her. "Who is it?" she called out in English. Whoever it was, started to answer in heavily accented English and then gave up rather limply. He had a much lower voice than anyone she knew.

"Who is it?" she asked again, this time in Swahili.

"A fundi to check a leak in the bathroom. May I come in?"

"Oh yes." she said, "I'll be right there." She put on her jacket again and went to the door. To be sure of who he was, she left the chain on, but opened the door a crack. There was a man in Ngong Hotel workman clothing who stooped down to pick up a basket full of tools. She took off the door chain. the man walked past her into the room. She closed the door and started to turn toward him, when to her horror his arm was around her neck, choking off any sound she might try to make. He yanked her violently toward the window. She dragged her feet and tried to fight him off with her arms but was no match for the much stronger and larger man. She could hardly breathe with his arm pushing into her windpipe.

When they reached the window, he bent forward and with one hand tried to push aside the drapery. He began to feel for the latch to open the window. Melissa realized that this would be her only chance and kicked him as hard as she could while he was off balance. His grip around her neck was less as he concentrated on feeling for the latch. She twisted around as much as possible and with both arms, she pushed him with all her strength through the already open window.

He screamed and the scream continued as he fell. Melissa sank to the floor, feeling faint and sick. Finally, she got shakily to her knees and looked out the open window.

There was great confusion below—she could see the fundi on the pavement. She saw no blood but she knew, of course that he was dead. She felt grateful that no one else had been hurt. She watched for a few seconds and then did something she always wondered about later. She went into the bathroom and washed her hands, face and neck. She applied fresh makeup and brushed her hair.

Then she went to the phone and asked to be put

through to the police commissioner. "May I speak to Commissioner Ngowi?" she asked when she had the police department on the line.

"Who may I say is calling?'"

"Melissa Lopes. I have important news."

"Just one moment, please," and then the Commissioner's voice came on.

"This is Melissa Lopes. About five minutes ago," she began, and her voice sounded so strange to her that she cleared her throat, took a deep breath and began again.

"About five minutes ago, Paul Mwenzaka came to my hotel room door. He said he was a workman come to repair a leak in the bathroom. I let him in, not realizing who he was. He grabbed me from behind as I was closing the door after him, and he dragged me by the neck to the window. I was unable to call for help and the door was closed anyway. He pulled me backward toward the window and intended to throw me out of it. He didn't know that I had turned off the air conditioning and opened the windows wide. But I had pulled the draperies closed again because I intended to change clothing. When he pulled the drapery aside to unlatch the window, he was bent forward. Before he discovered that the windows were open, I kicked him with all my strength, he let go of my neck to regain balance and then I pushed as hard as I could push – he fell out of the window."

"Good God! What floor are you on?"

"The fifteenth."

"Was anyone else hurt by his fall?"

"No. But there are many people crowded around him now. I am sorry. I didn't want to do it but I had to."

"I understand. Lock your door. Let no one in. No one. Do you understand? I'll be right over."

"Thank you, goodbye..." She hung up and went to the door and checked the lock.

Then she sat down in an armchair and thought she would cry, but there were no tears at all. Just sadness. That was the fundi who had been so helpful to her, bringing the muslin so her materials wouldn't get dirty, going off for scissors. She had liked him and he had no reason to dislike her. She sat still and grieved.

She was still sitting there, her hands folded quietly on her lap, but her thoughts as wild as squirrels in a cage, darting from one idea to another, trying to make some sense out of all the violence.

A loud rap on the door and a strong voice called out, "Miss Lopes, I am Commissioner Ngowi."

"Yes, Commissioner," She hurried to the door and opened it.

"The ambulance is down there. The police have taken pictures, and the newspapers have, too. Mwenzaka will be taken to the morgue now." He explained all this as he came in, being careful to lock the door behind him.

Melissa remained standing, unsure of whether he would want to take her to the station and talk to her there, or if he would do so right in the hotel room.

"My secretary is having a few words with the policeman at your door. He will be here in a few minutes and take down your statement and have you sign it. The policemen at the door are to make sure we won't be disturbed while you are speaking for the record." He went to the door then and let in a much younger officer who had a briefcase and portable typewriter. "Now, Miss Lopes just tell us exactly what happened from the very beginning and be sure to omit nothing."

Melissa told her story again. The officer typed it and then sat at the desk to transcribe notes into an official looking document.

"Can I send out for anything? A cup of tea. Perhaps?"

"No, thank you. I am fine, really. Just a bit shaken, I suppose."

"I wouldn't wonder! Our inquiries had already shown that Paul Mwenzaka had been going to a hoteli on the outskirts of the city that is known to be a gathering place for radicals. As soon as we were informed of the attempt on your life at the godown, and knew the name of the man, it was relatively easy to find his associates and to discover where he spent his time. Mr. Montero told me where you were and I thought you would be safe here. I was wrong, and I am sorry about that."

"You wouldn't have known I would be so foolish as to let him into my room. I didn't feel afraid to let in a fundi to work on the plumbing! In fact I was glad to see someone; he even had workman type clothes with a logo of the Ngong Hotel. There must be other radicals who helped him. Oh yes, he also had a basket full of plumbing tools. He bent down to pick them up just as I opened the door a crack, and I didn't see his face at all until he was in the room."

The Commissioner got up and walked about restlessly waiting for his secretary to finish typing up a clean copy of Melissa's statement. He opened the draperies and looked out on the crowd that had gathered. "Ghouls!" he snapped and closed the drapery, disgusted by the curious crowd milling about below.

"The barkeep at the hoteli admits that Paul Mwenzaka often spoke against your cousin whom he had hated for a long time. He denies that Paul ever said a harsh word about anyone else. Of course, he also says that his place isn't a gathering place for racists and political extremists and that he doesn't know who else might be involved in the murders. I don't believe him. We have men out there who will question all the regular trade. We will find out who Mwenzaka was with that night. For all we know, the others may think that Paul already told someone."

By now there was constant noise in the hall. The policeman at the door was instructed earlier to let no one even knock and he was insisting that the newsmen be orderly and wait patiently, but he wasn't having much success.

The electric typewriter was clicked off, and the statement handed to Melissa to read over and to sign. A copy was given to the Police commissioner who scanned it and satisfied himself that the information was as he had heard it, Melissa read her copy very carefully and then took the pen the policeman handed her and wrote her name on the line he indicated. She thought about waiting for Mr. Mathers, but she knew that what she had said was the truth and that she wouldn't change it for any reason.

"Miss Lopes, if you would like to go into the bathroom and lock the door, I will let the newsmen in. They will want to take pictures from the window and they need to know what happened. I will tell them and spare you that." He motioned for her to go. He raised his body of fifteen stone or more into a standing position of six feet and slowly went to the door and opened it to let in a throng of clamoring newsmen. They jostled each other to get to the window and take shots of the street below; they took photos of the Police Commissioner whose facial expression had become anything but benevolent and they all demanded to know where the occupant of the room was, and was it really Melissa Lopes and how had the fundi fallen from the window? No one seemed willing to listen; each had another question. The Commissioner stood there and listened to them and finally asked for silence. Suddenly they all went quiet at once and took out pens or pencils to copy down whatever he would say.

He told the story just as Melissa had told it to him, and he also gave the account of the attempt on her life at the godown.

Melissa leaned against the bathroom door listening and smiled wryly to herself at the stir she had created.

"All my life I have been the kind of girl who obeys her parents, tries hard at school and gets on well with others. I always had gold stars on my school reports and threw my candy wrappers into the dust bin— and now, I avoid getting murdered twice in one day and end up pushing someone out a fifteenth story window."

She was thinking of how strange it all was, when she was drawn from her reverie by the indignant roars the Police commissioner directed at a journalist.

"Your paper has daily articles urging Africans to demand expulsion of Asians. Hate drips from every line. Are you really so surprised when some of your readers murder whole families? That poor fundi believed he had no choice but to kill again to hide his involvement in the first murders. Oh yes, it is true that we have one less Asian family and one less Asian business, but have we gained anything?" The man didn't attempt to answer because Melissa heard nothing but a temporary silence which was followed by "Please let us talk to the girl" and calls of "Come out and talk to us."

Melissa thought she must seem ridiculous holed up in the bathroom and decided that if she didn't go out now, they would just camp on her doorstep until she did. So she turned the doorknob and walked out.

"Tell us what happened!"

"I told the police and Commissioner Ngowi has read you my statement. It is just as he read it."

"Was your dress soiled and ripped in the struggle here?"

"No, in the godown, on the floor there."

"The bump on your head?"

"When the bale of material hit me, or more likely, the trolley handle. I really don't know. The whole affair both here and there took place in just a few minutes."

"You have enough," said the PC and walked over and opened the door for the newsmen. "I will let you know just as soon as we have anything new to report in the case."

The reporters left and the Commissioner and his secretary weren't long in following.

Melissa sighed with relief when they left. She was glad it was over; it would have been unbearable to have them waiting for her at every turn.

She decided to take off the unlucky beige silk suit for good. She folded it carefully into her suitcase and chose another dress to wear after the hot shower she planned to take.

An hour later, the phone rang and Mathers said he had finished up at the godown and would be back soon to take her to dinner.

Melissa realized Mathers didn't know about Paul Mwenzaka. He seemed so matter of fact. She made herself comfortable on the bed with her skirt smoothed out carefully beneath her so as not to get wrinkled, turned the dials on the radio till she got a music program and tried to block everything else from her mind. It didn't work. Finally there was a knock and a voice saying, "Reginald Mathers here, are you ready, Melissa?"

"Right away." she called, picked up her purse and joined him in the hall.

"Unbelievable, simply unbelievable. Two attempts in one day. You lead a charmed life, how wonderfully fortunate for you that the windows were opened and that he didn't know it. I am proud of you, you could easily have been too frightened to act, but you took advantage of the one moment when you could prevail. Astounding!" Melissa didn't say a word. Mathers had just been informed of the attempt on her life at the hotel, and it certainly was being talked about. She looked up, smiled, and shrugged her shoulders as if to say it all seemed pretty astounding to her, too.

Mathers asked to be seated with Melissa where they would not be in full view. He handed her a menu and when she said she would just have a light meal because she had no desire to eat, even though she felt hungry.

He insisted on ordering the food for Melissa who smiled but shook her head as he told the maitre d'hotel that they would have shrimp cocktail to be followed by tilapia from the Nile and small beef fillets, assorted hot vegetables and a chocolate mousse.

"I shall do well if I finish the cocktail and coffee."

"You are hungry, you must eat."

And so she did.

CHAPTER ELEVEN

The next morning Melissa met Mathers at the door of her room at exactly 8:10 and after breakfast they took a taxi to Montero's office so they could sign the papers concerning the sale of the business. Sale of the merchandise was agreed on at 65% of its value and the government had agreed to rent the godown for one year with an option to buy. That was excellent news, too.

Montero invited them out for lunch and for a drive around the city so they could see some interesting new buildings and a new residential area. Melissa had sudden misgivings. "Is it all right for me to leave?"

"I asked about that." Mathers replied. "'You must keep yourself in readiness, in the event the police need you here. But the P.C. thinks that most unlikely. He sends you his best wishes for good fortune."

Since the flight back to Dar was during daylight hours, she enjoyed the sight of the great Rift Valley, Mount Kilimanjaro's snow capped peak and the little blue ribbon of the Nile.

"Kenya is so big, so empty, you would think there would be room for many more people here."

"It looks that way, doesn't it. And yet, much of it is already over-populated. There isn't enough rainfall, herders have to walk great distances just to find a bit of grass to keep their cows alive. The crops wither, the grass doesn't grow and the animals and the people die. A denser population would be tragic in most parts of East Africa, at least till some basic problems are solved."

"What could be done?"

"No one seems to know. The English Government had a very expensive scheme to raise groundnuts... the Americans call them peanuts, and they raise a lot of them there. Several missionaries and many African farmers tried to tell the English that you can't raise groundnuts in that area. But it was tried anyway because the protein in the nuts would be a great help to the African diet. The scheme failed. Good will doesn't make up for absence of rainfall.

"Manufacturing is out, not enough roads to transport goods and if roads were built what could be produced? Much of it is poor farm country and barely keeps herders alive. Mills and factories need something to produce and it is all a great circular problem and in the meantime, the people live very hard lives with much moving about. The children couldn't go to school even if there were more schools to go to."

"I suppose that is why Dar and Nairobi have so many people looking for work."

"Oh yes. And most really have no skills needed in cities. No wonder that some of them turn to robbery."

Dar es Salaam airport was announced and they prepared to leave the plane.

"You'd better take off your jacket, Melissa. It's cool in the plane but when you go out into that moist, hot air, you may faint."

They gathered up their things and walked down the ramp into the humidity of the tropic coast.

"Ah this feels good!" Melissa said happily.

"It always does to me, too. I go back to England to visit but I miss this hothouse atmosphere. Some people can't stand it, but I feel right at home in it. I'll be sorry if I have to leave. I called my house and the chauffeur will meet us. Your Tonio won't be out here till tonight and you can get in touch with him by phoning from the airport to his office."

They walked along companionably toward the baggage counter and customs check. Melissa said thoughtfully, "Perhaps now I won't have to leave either."

"Maybe not, but don't count on it, since the only certainty is that nothing is certain."

Mathers' chauffeur, errand boy and gardener, all wrapped into one in the person of a handsome Makonde tribesman with neat facial markings cut into his face was sleeping soundly- sprawled out on a wooden bench in front of the air terminal.

"How can anyone sleep through planes coming and going?" Mathers asked mainly to himself, as he bent down and shook his servant gently, "Suleimani, I'm home. Let's go."

Suleimani awoke, greeted them pleasantly, stood up and said, "The car is over here." He started off toward it.

They had to laugh at how quickly he woke up when he needed to and how soundly he slept through things that didn't concern him. The trip into town was easy since it was too early for people to be leaving work. They let her off at Gomes' as Suleimani helped her up the stairs with her suitcase and the large package of materials which Mathers had the foresight to bring along after the attempt on her life at the godown.

"I'll be in touch with you and you come to the office if you have any questions." Mathers called to her from the open window of the car.

"Thank you, I appreciate all you have done for me."

"Think nothing of it. It certainly made a change."

Melissa smiled and remembered the last time she had heard that particularly English expression. It was Fiona Richards' comment about staying in the Masai boma.

Mrs. Gomes was home and heard her coming so she had the door wide open.

"Welcome back!"

"It is good to be back, Mrs. Gomes. Asante, Suleimani!"

"Asante, Mama." he replied, already halfway down the stairs.

"I suppose you know you are in all the papers again?" Mrs. Gomes asked.

"I am not surprised. The pictures the photographers took in the hotel room, no doubt?"

"Yes, here." Mrs. Gomes handed her the paper. She looked at it and it seemed to be someone else—she shrugged her shoulders, tried to smile and set the paper down.

"I should have gone to Nairobi with you, then none of

this would have happened." Mrs. Gomes said sadly.

"I don't know. Maybe it would have happened and both of us might now be dead. What is over is over and we can't change it. I really wish it hadn't happened. I certainly never wanted to hurt anyone. I simply did not want to die myself. "

"You had no choice in what you did. God was looking after you."

"Yes, I believe that, but the fundi was also God's child. Wasn't He looking after him, too?"

"Perhaps He was. There are worse things than death of the body. If the fundi was repentant for the first crime, and that is certainly possible, then he may have been so frightened that he wasn't acting rationally in trying to silence you. God prevented him from committing another crime. It is also possible that he was unrepentant and chose to do evil rather than good. God does give us free will in the matter of sin, although in many other things we certainly have very little choice."

"Perhaps that is for our own good too?" Melissa asked.

"I think so. When our duty is clear and we have no real alternative, we are often able to be our best possible self. There is something about a life full of thousands of choices that very few of us can bear."

The ever practical Mrs. Gomes sighed, "Philosophy is fine, but food is too, so let's get something on the table before Tonio gets here. He sent a messenger over to tell me you called from the airport in Nairobi that you would be back this afternoon and I invited him for the evening meal."

Melissa set the table, and was combing her hair when she heard Tonio at the door. "I am never going to let that girl go to Nairobi again. The place is all bad news." Tonio complained to Mrs. Gomes. Melissa rushed out to greet him and then he pushed her to arms' length to look at her more closely. "Your eye?" he exclaimed with horror.

"Certainly is a deep shade of purple," she admitted.

"Oh well. never mind. I suppose it gives you a certain air. Your business affairs I hope went better than the rest of your stay?"

"Oh yes, everything is sold - merchandise, house and furnishings except for a few things that will be shipped to me here. A set of fine English china, four rings and several Persian carpets."

"I hope you don't have to pay duty on it at 100% of its value!" Tonio looked shocked as only a tax agent can look when he thinks someone has let himself in for a fantastically large tax.

"No, Tonio. Mr. Mathers has arranged for it to come in as our personal belongings, which of course they are. The inheritance tax has already been paid on it, so it's really all ours now."

"Ours?"

"Yes, our belongings. Everything we have will always belong to us both. Now we have good times to enjoy. Do you realize we can have a home built here in Dar? Perhaps right on the sea..."

Tonio didn't answer. Just looked pensive and Mrs. Gomes interrupted with, "Come right to the table, I have something you both like and I don't want food to get cold."

"Mmm, does it look good!" Tonio said. "I saw the paper before I went to work and it rather took my appetite. Haven't had anything but a banana all day long. Melissa looked like a forlorn bedraggled kitten and I felt guilty for not being with her."

Melissa laughed slightly and said, "You two have over-developed guilt complexes. If I have to be followed around all the time to prevent me from getting into trouble, we will need to hire a keeper, since I am too old for an ayah."

The meal was the famous Goan sor patel, steaming and rich and spicy, served with little plates of shockingly hot lime pickle.

"My, this is delicious. I like English food, but it often seems bland." said Melissa and Tonio nodded agreement.

"Well, you are Goan, by blood, if not by birth and in our homes we are accustomed to spicy food." Mrs. Gomes said.

"I wonder what other people really think Tonio and I are. We have never even visited in Asia, yet most people, I suppose, call us Asians. Our ancestors lived in Goa and were Goans. But we have never lived there and don't even speak Konkoni enough to carry on a conversation. And we don't speak enough Portuguese to matter much, although we have Portuguese names. We think we are Zanzibaris, but the Zanzibaris don't. Tanzania, by the way, told Mathers it will provide me with a passport, but I don't think they consider either of us really Tanzanians because we are not dark skinned enough to qualify."

They sat a long time over their coffee and Melissa filled them in on what was not in the paper.

After a pause, Tonio said, "I have some news too. Hated to ruin your homecoming or spoil a good meal. Actually, it isn't really such bad news, but you might not like it much."

Melissa looked at him afraid to ask any question at all. Finally Mrs. Gomes said, "Tell us. The suspense is probably worse than the news."

"You both remember that I have mentioned that our office here is short handed, but not so much that we can't get our work done. In the Nairobi office there are still a few Englishmen seconded from the British tax service. Uganda, however, recently lost several men and urgently needs help. Dar office is sending me to Uganda. It will be for at least a year and perhaps for much longer."

"Do you have to accept it?" Melissa asked.

"Yes, I think I do. If I decide not to go to Kampala, I may well find myself out of work, although I am needed here too."

Mrs. Gomes said calmly, "Kampala is beautiful, I have been there many times because I have relatives there. I used to have more, but most have gone to UK. No reason to think that this is bad news, Tonio. Men get transfers all the time."

"Will you come too, Melissa?" Tonio asked in a soft voice.

"Of course. When do we leave?"

"I have to leave tomorrow on the evening flight."

Melissa looked confused, but was about to say she would be ready. Mrs. Gomes broke in and said firmly, "Melissa will go out to see you off at the airport. She will need to collect her baptismal record, some money must be deposited in a bank in Kampala and that will mean a visit to Mathers and phone calls to Kenya, at the very least. You must realize that she can't get married in church without her Baptismal record and she will need a visa for Uganda. You will be supplied with one, but she isn't employed by the East African Community and you aren't married yet. I just don't see how all that can be arranged by tomorrow evening."

"Mrs. Gomes, you are right again," said Tonio with a sigh. "When do you suppose Melissa could join me in Kampala?"

"I suppose that we could be there in a week or two. I hope you notice I said we. It is time I visited my cousins there, and I don't think much of the idea of you two trying to get settled into a new job and a new home in another country without someone else along to help get a wedding together soon after we arrive." Mrs Gomes began to look less authoritative and more dreamy, which probably meant that she was making wedding plans.

"I brought back lovely satin for a wedding gown," Melissa added hopefully.

"Good. We will take it to a dressmaker right away. Tonio, you just do a good job at the office. Now, you two go out for a walk and I will deal with these dishes and get plans under way. While you are out, be sure to visit Father Ciprian and tell him you need your Baptismal and perhaps Communion and Confirmation records too. Tell him you plan to be married in two weeks and he will be sure to have them ready for Melissa to take when we leave for Kampala."

On the way over to the White Fathers' residence, Tonio said, "I feel better since Mrs. Gomes got into this. I knew about the transfer for only three days, just since you left I made arrangements to sell my car to a chap at the office. He will drive me out to the airport and then take possession of the car. I will hate to lose it."

"I will too, since I will have a long walk home from the airport on the Pugu road!" "Not to worry, he will drive you back to Gomes'." Tonio chuckled.

Father Ciprian told them he hoped to have everything ready in a day because he already had the school and church records from Zanzibar. "I have been following your career through the newspapers, Melissa. I must say that you are interesting copy. I've thought about you and you've been remembered in all my masses." "Thank you, Father. I feel sure that your prayers were helpful. My escapes seem almost miraculous."

The priest blessed them and wished them success in their new home. "Never despair, God sends us few crosses, those we must accept. Most of our burdens come from other people and God allows them to happen. We can struggle against those and we must always struggle to make this life better not only for ourselves but for all mankind." He was interrupted then by an African who needed help so they excused themselves and promised to write.

cut

Melissa went alone to Mathers' office the next morning and was paging through an ancient and well-thumbed magazine when Mathers looked into the waiting room and said, "Come in, Melissa. I just had Nairobi on the phone. Montero says everything is going as planned." He rubbed his hands together appreciatively and motioned her to a comfortable leather chair and seated himself behind a beautiful large desk made of heavy African mninga wood.

"What brings you here today?" he asked like a kindly uncle.

"Tonio has been transferred to Uganda. The Kampala office. It will be for at least a year and he leaves on today's flight. I will join him next week, so we will be married there. I wonder if it would be possible to have some money transferred from the bank in Kenya to one in Kampala so that I can buy the things we need to set up housekeeping?"

Mathers didn't answer immediately. She looked so happy and he didn't like to throw cold water on her enthusiasm.

"Melissa, I am afraid to take the money out of a Kenyan bank and put it into one in Uganda. There are beginning to be such awful currency exchange problems. I don't want you to lose anything. We already have arranged to have a few thousand pounds put into the bank here. You could always lose that too, I suppose, but somehow I feel safer with at least part of it in Dar es Salaam. I never advise any of my clients to break the law, but it is getting difficult not to, especially with Asian clients. Let us just suppose everything were put into the account in Kampala and the Ugandans decided to throw all Asians out. I wish I knew how to advise you. I really don't."

"I have heard of people taking money out and putting it into English banks. They buy diamonds and smuggle the diamonds out too, or buy lots of gold bangles."

Mathers grinned. "Yes, I know the type. The women wear large diamonds in their noses and the older women are bent double with money belts around their waist and every so often someone is caught and loses everything. It looks to me like the East African Tax Community is breaking up. These three countries are in such different stages of development, there are strong tribal rivalries, and varying ideas of what should be done with scarce revenues."

"And Tonio is going to Kampala as a tax agent for the East African Community! Will his job even be safe?"

"It should be. After all, how many senior auditors do any of these three countries have that are citizens? Tonio is a Tanzanian, well educated, able, and hard working.

It costs far more to hire men from overseas who just get reasonably adjusted to the country, the climate, the system and their tours of duty are over. I wish Tonio were going to Australia, for instance, but if you went there, I can't imagine how we could get your money out at all. Two thousand pounds is all you would be allowed to take out."

"A few short weeks ago, it would have seemed like a fortune to me."

"Yes. I suppose so, and yet, now that you have it, it would be depressing to let one of these three governments take it with no compensation at all. As it is, a great deal was paid to death duties, for the police protection of the house since that dreadful night, to mention nothing at all of my fees nor those of your uncle's solicitor, Mr. Montero."

"Yes, I realize that. I would certainly like to pay you now, if I can."

"I'll make out a bill and you can write me a check for it on your bank here. But I think you had better retain me as your solicitor for a while longer in case things don't work out well in Kampala."

"I will, because I don't know what I would have done without you. And what of Montero's bill?"

"Pay it as soon as you get it. Use your bank account in Kenya. It is likely to be a rather hefty sum, but he had unusual expenses too. I would expect his fee will be both high and honest. He will be in touch with me, and I shall keep him informed of your whereabouts. It is necessary that I always know where you live, naturally."

"Mrs. Gomes has been kind enough to say she will accompany me to Kampala.

She has relatives there that she wants to see and she

is eager to put on a real wedding for me. There won't be anyone to attend – but you know Mrs. Gomes!"

"I do indeed. A lovely woman. You are fortunate she is going with you. Her help will be invaluable."

"Yes, she is like a second mother to me."

"When you arrive in Kampala, why don't you stay at the Grand Hotel until you find a house you like. I will know where you are and it is pleasant. The food is excellent and it's in a good location for you. There is a newer and more elegant hotel, but it is one of those skyscraper affairs. I think you might prefer the Grand."

Melissa nodded, thinking of her last experience in a high rise hotel.

Tonio came by after work and she was ready for her last ride in his VW. "I will always remember this little car. How glad I was to see you in it that wonderful day on the beach at Silver Sands."

"To me you were like a treasure washed up by the sea. When I was a little boy, I used to like to look out to sea and dream of enchanted kingdoms under the sea. I will never forget the way you looked running toward me, your hair still wet and streaming behind you. I looked out to sea, and there was a dhow headed toward Dar Harbor. Even before you told me how you got in, I'd guessed it was by dhow. Our grandchildren will tell that story. It is certainly not the usual court-ship. For one thing, our parents chose us for each other. It was so perfect and for me it couldn't have been more romantic. Just because we were chosen for each other doesn't make it unromantic. But we certainly haven't found it easy to get married!"

"I said my goodbyes to the Richards and to Mathers. He advised me to stay at the Grand Hotel until we find an apartment in Kampala. I think I would like a house, a place we can call our very own. He says that a transfer of funds can be arranged from a Nairobi bank to Kampala so we can buy what we need."

"I feel guilty having my wife provide everything."

"Well, don't. If we were still on Zanzibar and things were the way they once were, my father would have helped us buy a house and our relatives would have helped us furnish it. We both have lost so much. Just be grateful now, not guilty."

Tonio's flight was soon called and he kissed her and held her close as she promised to be in Kampala in a week. His co-worker who had bought the car, arrived with another man and said he would be glad to drive her back into town. So she rode in the little VW once more.

The young African was talkative, pleasant, and commented that he hoped Tonio would enjoy Kampala and an advancement would perhaps come easier in Uganda.

"Tonio is glad of the opportunity, I suppose, but I think he would have preferred to stay in his own country."

"In India?" the black man asked in surprise.

"Why no, in Tanzania. Neither he nor his parents ever saw India," she answered.

"Ah." Said the African, rather perplexed.

They talked about many things on the way in, but

in the back of Melissa's mind was the fact that an African who personally liked Tonio could not really accept him as a citizen of Tanzania. If he couldn't what about those who didn't know him? Not a pleasant thought.

The wedding gown and veil were ready in three days time and on the fourth a messenger came from Father Ciprian carrying her records and Tonio's.

She phoned Mathers from the chemist's shop on the corner to tell him when she and Mrs. Gomes were leaving and he insisted on driving them to the airport.

She intended to shake his hand before boarding the plane, but instead she threw both arms around his neck and kissed him, and tears came unbidden at having to leave such a good friend. Then she hurried up the stairway onto the plane. followed by a laughing Mrs. Gomes.

"I don't know what got into me. I just think so much of him...Oh, dear me, Mathers of all people. I suppose he almost died of mortification."

"Why no. He didn't. He blushed beetroot red, but he looked delighted."

Mathers stood on the observation deck and waved and she waved back. "I think I shall never see him again."

"Don't think that, Melissa. Life brings back people we think we will never see again, and it takes away those we expect never to lose. We can't know. I am old enough to admit that, and even to believe there is a pattern to it. Even though I certainly don't see the pattern. By the way, what is in that pretty package?"

Melissa opened it and found it contained two box-es, one a large box of Italian chocolates which made her smile remembering how Mathers had recognized her sweet tooth, and the other was *Cookery For The Beginner.*

Melissa spotted Tonio as soon as she left the plane in Kampala. She ran toward him calling over her shoulder to Mrs. Gomes that she would join her at the baggage section.

Tonio was smiling delightedly, he said, "This has been a long week. I thought you would never get here!"

Melissa caught him up on all her news and he told her he'd found a good estate agent who would take them around to see what was on the market. "I'm in a boarding house not far from the Grand Hotel. The woman rents rooms by the week or month and it is clean enough. You will like the Grand Hotel and they say that the food is very good indeed."

"Haven't you sampled it?" Asked Mrs. Gomes.

"No. I always feel ill at ease eating alone. English-men don't mind, but then, I am not English."

"The three of us will be dining together tonight and we'll all enjoy it."

"Oh good. I have about had my fill of cassava, ugali (corn porridge) and bananas."

"That reminds me that Mr. Mathers gave us a wed-ding present of a cookery book."

"Something else I failed to consider. I suppose you are a real beginner and that I shall have to eat a great deal of scorched food and half done biscuits?"

"I hope not, but I wouldn't be surprised."

The estate agent showed them houses and one of them was so much like the ones they had grown up in that they knew it was what they wanted.

The old couple who lived there hated to part with it, but it had become too much for them. Melissa was able to buy much of the furniture in the house also and that was a great help since everything had been made especially for the place it occupied.

"Now we can go and see the priest and tell him the wedding can be this Saturday.

You can buy kitchen equipment and bedding and on Saturday at last we can be married."

Kampala, Uganda. The newly built Apollo Hotel (built by the then president of Uganda – Milton Obote) and next to it at the bottom right hand side the lovely Grand Hotel which figures in our story as the place the wedding party took place. (Circa 1969)

Scene of downtown Kampala, Uganda (Circa 1969)

CHAPTER TWELVE

M rs. Gomes was glad to hear that the wedding would be soon, but her worry was that she wouldn't have enough time to get a real reception together.

"Do you think it is necessary to have a party afterward?" Melissa asked a bit uneasily, "After all, no one will know us."

"They won't know you afterward either unless you invite them now. I want you two to start off your married life with a few people whom you consider possible friends, or at the very least, acquaintances you respect. Marriage is not a private affair. There will be children brought into the world and other people will have to deal with them whether they are brought up well or not. New mouths to be fed, whether or not the parents can feed them and whether the country is rich or poor. Marriage concerns us all."

"Where will this party take place?" Tonio asked mildly giving in to the inevitable.

"Right here in the hotel dining room. I have spoken to the manager and he says I have only to inform him of the time and he can arrange for plenty of savouries, cakes and coffee. This wedding party will be my gift to you both!"

"Mrs. Gomes, you have done so much for us already, I can never repay you. It would be wonderful if your gift could be arranging the wedding and reception, but let the bill be sent to me...please."

"Well, all right. I believe I understand. Now Tonio, how many do you think might attend from your office?"

"Perhaps twenty—including husbands and wives."

"Fine, and I have about ten relatives, including children. I shall arrange for thirty and if more come, the manager can easily attend to it. By the way, what did you plan to do about a best man?"

"I never thought about it. I don't know anyone here well enough to ask!"

"Well, I plan to be matron of honor. I have brought with me a pale green lace I wore to a wedding last year, just the thing! Now, in regard to the best man, I have a cousin here who is a very nice middle-aged man. A Goan, a citizen of Uganda and I know he owns a good blue suit. Don't you think he would do?"

"Certainly, if you think he wouldn't mind giving up a Saturday for a total stranger."

"I felt sure you would need him, so I asked him. He said he would be delighted and if you have someone else, he will forget I ever mentioned it. If you want to call and 'confirm his appointment' here is the number where he can be reached tomorrow."

Tonio took the card, thanked her and said, "Do you realize that next Saturday after the reception we can move into our new home?"

"Well, as for me, I will stay here Saturday night and Sunday I will visit with relatives. They will take me to the airport. Now if you two will excuse me, I still have things to attend to, flowers, newspapers, caterers..."

"Do you get the feeling Tonio, that we are 'Babes in the Woods?'"

"Sometimes. Mrs. Gomes is like a grey haired guardian angel."

Next day Melissa bought kitchen tools and bedding. It was fun for her to go with her matron of honor and order flowers and discuss food and beverages with the staff at the hotel. She enjoyed it all.

Mrs. Gomes asked, "Do you have any misgivings at all, Melissa?"

"No!"

"It would be very natural. Most girls do. I know I had hysterics, and a friend of mine tried to run away from home..."

"Why did she do that, wasn't she in love?"

"Oh yes. She has been happily married for many years. But sudden misgivings aren't unusual."

"I used to think about it, you know, whether I really wanted to marry him or not. But that was years ago. I believe that this was meant to be. Neither of us has anyone else, our parents wanted it, we have always been attracted to each other, and we have both been through so much. I feel like he is a part of me. He seems like a husband, but also like a friend or brother, and best of all, I'm in love with him."

In the morning, Mrs. Gomes' cousin and her husband arrived to take them to the church. The husband sat on a chair by the window and smoked an immense black cigar to entertain himself while the hairdresser rearranged Melissa's hair a little. Mrs.

Gomes and the cousin saw to the placement of the headdress and veil and Melissa thought to herself, "I could fall sound asleep now, but as long as I stay on on my feet, no one would notice a thing. It is all out of my hands." Oddly it was a comforting thought.

In a great gust of cigar smoke, they finally got into the car and left for church. To protect the ladies' hair, the windows weren't rolled down and the cigar smoke became very thick and Melissa began to giggle. This didn't seem to surprise anyone, it was considered perfectly natural for a bride to be a bit nervous. The church was lovely with the flowers they had ordered and the organist began the wedding march right on time. Melissa could see Tonio standing at the front of the church with the cousin's husband at his side.

Melissa asked suddenly, "Who shall I walk down the aisle with?"

"You will walk alone, just like a queen. I will be right behind you."

For the first time, Melissa felt a bit of sadness, she missed her father, He would have been proud of her in her lovely dress, marrying Tonio whom he'd always liked.

She caught her breath, and then in time with the music, she proceeded slowly and regally down the long aisle clasping her bouquet of white roses, her eyes fixed on Tonio who was watching her come toward him. The look on his face unfortunately was pure fright.

"Why he is as nervous as I am!"

Finally she joined him at the altar and together

they walked up the two steps toward the priest. Melissa was shaking and beginning to feel a bit faint. Tonio bent down slightly and said sweetly. "You smell just like a strong cigar."

She had to smile, her nervousness completely gone. She looked up at Tonio and could see that he was at ease now, too. Nothing like a strong cigar, she thought.

All afternoon Mrs. Gomes was in her element, she saw to everything, no one was left alone and everyone had plenty to eat and drink. A general feeling of good will permeated the hotel dining room. Melissa and Tonio enjoyed the party too and marveled at the number of people that had come to wish them well.

Finally Mrs. Gomes said it would be proper for them to leave so that the other guests would feel free to leave also.

Melissa kissed her and said, "I can't ever say what I feel in my heart for you. We will meet again won't we?"

"Probably, next year in Dar!"

Tonio who had known her longer than Melissa, was also emotional at saying goodbye. To help him Mrs. Gomes said, "Tonio, don't you know yet that people turn up when you least expect them?" She kissed them and shooed them off to the car. The guests followed them out and someone had a basketful of rose petals which were thrown at them. Melissa took careful aim and tossed her bouquet to a little girl who was still jumping up and down gleefully as they drove off.

"Does it seem to you that we should be going somewhere, like to a resort or something?" Tonio asked.

"It seems to me that I will be delighted to go to our own home and get out of this gown. I like the way it looks, but long sleeves are hot, and this hairdo. What a relief to let it down."

Tonio agreed, "I will take off the tie and jacket—just think, alone at last. You are right, there isn't anywhere we could be happier tonight than in our home."

CHAPTER THIRTEEN

An old African couple, Hassani and Amina, employed by the former owners, stayed on. Melissa liked having the wife in the house during the day and her husband continued to keep the garden beautifully green and luxurious. Flowers bloomed in profusion and life was wonderful.

Or so it seemed. Suddenly the President of Uganda, Milton Obote, was overthrown and a military government took control.

"Tonio, I am afraid it is all starting over again. If the military seizes power, it can do anything else it wants to do, can't it?"

Tonio didn't answer at once, and then he said slowly, "What I am most worried about now is that Tanzania hasn't recognized this government and we are Tanzanians. I am needed back there too, but Tanzania hasn't asked to have me back. I suppose I will just stay at work here, but I can't help but feel uncomfortable."

The months from March till August went along without much change in their lives, everyone treated them well and Tonio went about his work as before.

Then in August, fighting was reported on the border, and in September Uganda accused Tanzania of bombing Ugandan villages. The city of Mwanza in Tanzania was bombed by Uganda. Feeling was running very high, at least among the native people. The Asians, the English and other Europeans simply deplored the whole affair and had no feeling against either county. If anything, they blamed Uganda for the mess, since Idi Amin, the General who had seized power, didn't seem fully in command of common sense, to put the matter charitably.

So it came as no surprise when Tonio came home one day and said, "Melissa, we ought to try to sell the house and we'd better leave the country, too. I know that many people have already been killed for disagreeing or seeming to, with Idi Amin."

She didn't want to distress Tonio any more than he already was, so she went out to the garden and picked a bouquet of flowers. The tears streamed from her eyes as she walked among the plants and flowers. This was coming to an end too, just as life on her dear Zanzibar had ended. It seemed that modern life was not to include people like them.

She dried her eyes and went into the house, arranged the flowers and brought them back to where Tonio was still sitting. He was not reading, nor looking at anything, just deep in thought.

The house was put up for sale, but no one was interested. The estate agent that had sold it to them had left for UK. The Asians with money to buy, had gone also, or were afraid to invest money in Uganda. The English were fewer every day.

"Let's try to rent it, Tonio. Perhaps as a home for some ambassador from overseas."

"I thought of that, but when the U.S. official was

beaten and the U.S. Government told its citizens not to travel through Uganda, I realized that there is going to be very little hope of renting it. There are still Asian countries who have embassies here and African countries that have good relations with Amin already have embassies and houses. But we can try. I will ask at the Libyan embassy today if they would like an extra residence. They are great friends of the present government, and they have plenty of oil money. I may have to be a bit late tonight, if I stop there on the way home. So don't worry."

Melissa didn't worry at first, but then it got to be eight o'clock and then nine, and still no Tonio. Dinner was very cold and dried out. She sat down and tried to eat something, but felt too frightened to eat anything.

Her African maid was sitting in front of her own little house in back. Melissa went down to talk to her and ask if by chance the phone had rung while she was in the garden, "Did Tonio call? Did anyone leave a message at the gate?"

"No. No one, Mem Sahib." She called to her husband and they spoke in Kikuyu, so Melissa couldn't understand.

Finally, the old man said in Swahili, "I will go to your husband's office and see what I can learn."

Melissa told him that Tonio had planned to go to the Libyan Embassy also. She gave him plenty of money for taxis and decided she wanted to go with him. The old man was very determined to go alone and seemed afraid to have her along. His wife was horrified at the idea of Melissa going out and they seemed to know or to feel that something was greatly amiss. Melissa thought she had best trust their intuition.

She sat in the lounge of her own house, paging through magazines whose pictures and words were no more than a blur to her. Her hands and feet felt cold although the house was warm. She made a cup of tea. Time was standing still.

Finally a taxi stopped in the driveway and the old servant got out. When the car was out of sight, he hurried into the house and said, "Oh Mem Sahib, I am very sorry, but Bwana is in a camp. Someone said he is an enemy of the people. They put him in a camp. Took his car. I ask for him at camp. He's not hurt, not sick, very fine." He added the last to have something good to report.

Shocked, she went to the phone and called the African who was in charge at Tonio's office. She told him what she knew and he told her there was nothing at all that he could do for her. He added that as a member of the Baganda tribe he was already out of favor with the new regime and feared his help would be worse than nothing. He suggested a solicitor who might be able to advise her in the morning.

But Melissa phoned the man immediately and he agreed to come to her home early in the morning. He would do what he could to get Tonio released, he refused to go out at night. Melissa didn't undress; she took a blanket and tried to sleep on the sofa. Finally she gave that up and just waited for the solicitor.

Soon after seven he arrived. It was obvious he was

no competition for Mr. Mathers.

He was much younger and less self assured. But he was black, and that might well make all the difference. Melissa welcomed him with great relief and they sat at the dining room table to discuss what could be done.

"I don't want to frighten you. No, no, not to frighten. Perhaps it is a good plan to have tickets out of the country. You see, Mama, although there is rule of law in this country, these are strange times. If we go out to the detention camp and can't get your husband released by any usual means, then perhaps we can get him out by showing the tickets for England.. I just don't know. I wish I could guarantee, but I must be honest with you. We go now?"

She went upstairs and put all the hundred shilling notes that she had into a small bundle and pinned it inside her blouse, her checkbook and the rest of her money went into her purse. She told the servants what she knew and that she would be back as soon as she could.

First they went to BOAC and there she bought two tickets to England. "May I speak to the manager?" She asked the clerk.

"Why yes. Back this way."

As soon as the manager rose from behind his desk she explained her position to him and asked if she might use his phone to call Mr. Mathers in Tanzania. She handed him a bill to pay for the call but he refused it. The operator rang several times; the call didn't go through. She realized how important it was that someone outside know where she and Tonio were, especially since it was possible that she would also be detained.

She asked the English manager of BOAC if he would contact Mr. Mathers in Tanzania or failing that, try to speak to Mr. Montero in Nairobi and read what she had written on a note. She left their addresses and phone numbers. The African solicitor was becoming very restive waiting for her and she was eager to go out to the detention camp. The manager of BOAC was very matter of fact, but assured her that he would "do the needful." That oddly English phrase reassured her more than anything else would have.

They drove in silence out to the detention camp. Melissa was shocked beyond belief to see it, to hear it, to smell it. The place was full of people, men, women and even children. There were terrible sounds of beatings, cries, screams and moans.

She looked at the African who simply shrugged his shoulders helplessly.

He has known all along about this place. That is why he has so little hope of getting Tonio and going back to town. As she thought this, her fear mounted and her hands went clammy. Her throat was so dry she couldn't swallow.

A guard stopped them and the African addressed him courteously in the same language. She understood that the guard knew Tonio by the sudden light in his eye when the solicitor described him. The guard looked calculatingly at Melissa and motioned for them both to follow him. About one hundred yards down the field he stopped at a concrete building much like the others, and went up to a window which had no glass, only iron bars. He called out for Antonio da Silva in a sharp, authoritative voice. In a moment Tonio appeared at the window. Melissa was sickened by what she saw. His eyes were blackened and there were purplish red bruises on his face where he had been struck. He obviously was holding himself up by hanging onto the bars. But he smiled when he saw her.

The African spoke to the guard, and then he asked Melissa to show the tickets for UK. The guard motioned for her to come with him, the solicitor, and Tonio to the office of the camp supervisor.

The office was empty except for a desk, one chair and a pompous officer whose uniform barely stretched across his fat belly. His feet were up on the desk and he was wiggling his fat brown toes.

Her African counsel asked him in English what the charge was.

"The blood sucking enemies of the people are now getting their just punishment for years of mistreating us." He recited this like a schoolboy who knows the words but not a shred of an idea of what it means.

Her counsel then suggested that it must be a case of mistaken identity because Antonio da Silva was an employee of the government itself, and much trusted and respected. Facts which could easily be ascertained by one simple telephone call to the ministry where he works.

The officer appeared uneasy. He clearly had not expected this.

Tonio looked terrible, and if he was really an employee of the government, the officer himself might be in trouble for having Tonio detained and beaten.

Melissa spoke up. "We have tickets to leave Uganda, Bwana, and passports in order. Couldn't you just let us leave the country?"

She didn't have to add that then no one would have a chance to punish him for his indiscriminate rounding up of Asians and for his bestial treatment of them. With a great swagger, as if he were doing her a courtesy which she didn't really deserve, he said, "Oh take him and go. He is of no use to the country anyway."

The solicitor and Melissa supported Tonio between them and started out of the office. Tonio paused after a few steps and asked, "Where is my car?" He had to repeat the question because his lips were swollen and his words indistinct.

"What car?" asked the officer with a smirk, "That Fiat out there is my car."

Tonio said nothing and the three of them with Tonio half carried by the other two, got into the African's VW and drove off. The rule of law was no more in Uganda and none of them knew when it might be allowed to return.

"What do we owe you?" Melissa asked as they parked in front of her own house.

"Oh, two hundred shillings." She was about to pay him in bills and then thought better of it and paid him by check. She was already afraid that Asians might not be able to withdraw money and the African would have a better chance than she would.

He looked at the check she handed him, and smiled ruefully, put it into his pocket and said sincerely, "I wish you good fortune."

The two servants came hurrying out when they heard the car drive up and they helped Tonio out of the car and into the house. Both were talking excitedly and were angry with what they saw. They helped her get him into bed and then she phoned a doctor who lived not far from their house.

"Please doctor, can you come right over? My husband has been beaten. He is here in bed, I know you are busy, but if you could try to come to him?"

The doctor, also an Asian, recognized her voice and said simply, "I'll be right there, Melissa."

She felt some sense of relief. The man servant sat by Tonio's bed and the woman was already in the kitchen preparing a pot of tea and scrambling eggs.

"Bwana no eat long time," she said.

Melissa was about to go back upstairs when she heard the sound of a car coming to a sudden stop in her driveway. A hand brake was pulled up sharply and the car door opened. She went to her front door and the young doctor was already there and asking, "Where is he?"

"Upstairs, come with me."

"How did it happen?" He asked angrily.

"The police arrested him and beat him after work last night when he stopped for a traffic sign."

"Any reason given?"

"Yes, that he is an Asian, an exploiter of the people,

a blood sucker."

Tonio was lying in bed with his knees drawn up and pajama legs rolled back exposing his legs full of welts and bruises and dried blood.

The doctor shook his head disgustedly, took off his jacket and opened his black bag. He listened first to Tonio's heart and lungs, examined his eyes, his ears and had him move different parts of his body.

"Bring me a basin of warm water, soap, a washcloth and towel."

Melissa hurried off to get them while Tonio and the doctor talked.

"You aren't the first patient I've attended that this has happened to. You are the first one the police themselves have beaten, but beatings are getting very common. You were wise not to appear in my office in this shape."

"Yes, we know. We are Zanzibaris. We have lived through this kind of thing. We know that the sight of blood just drives some people crazy. Even if they would not have committed the original crime, they can't seem to resist adding to it."

"So true...Reminds me of chickens pecking to death any other chicken that has a speck of blood showing. I think you are all right internally, doesn't seem to be any bleeding and there are no broken bones. I'll give you something to put on your cuts that will prevent infection and I imagine you'll be fine in a few days, though a bit stiff."

"Thank you, doctor," Tonio said but his voice sounded as though he couldn't imagine anything being fine in a day or so.

"Several of us in the Asian community have an appointment to see Idi Amin this afternoon to discuss the condition of the Asians that are remaining here. After all, many of us are Ugandan citizens and have nowhere to go. What will become of the people that depend on our services? Who will care for my patients?" He answered his own question. "Many of them will die unattended and sooner than they should have."

Tonio said, "I don't think meeting with Idi Amin will do any good. It will just give him a forum for more wild talk."

"I hope you are wrong."

"I do too. But if mental illness doesn't come upon one suddenly, does mental health appear out of nowhere?"

The doctor didn't answer, but packed up his instruments and put on his suit coat and asked, "Will you stay here in Uganda?"

"No." Tonio replied firmly. And then, almost playfully he asked, "Would you like to buy a nice house, completely furnished and equipped?" The doctor grinned, shook his head and left the room.

Melissa followed him downstairs and asked what she owed him.

"I'll mail you a bill."

"Indeed. A bill. In care of general delivery, perhaps?"

"Perhaps. Good luck to you both."

"Thank you. I will remember you and the others..."

Melissa took a bowl of bananas and a box of English biscuits and went upstairs to have breakfast with Tonio who had already eaten the breakfast the maid had prepared.

"Didn't they feed you at all in there?"

"Oh yes. We had ugali, but I couldn't move my lips then and felt quite a pronounced lack of appetite. I wish there was something I could do for the people that are still in that camp. I suppose there will be more of them every day. I used to wonder if I should have studied law, but if a country doesn't want a rule of law, then no amount of legal experience can help much. I think that most Ugandans would be shocked to see that camp..."

"Yes, but then, we never thought that Karume would last in Zanzibar either.

Apparently those that were shocked were powerless to do anything, or they died trying...or they left the Island. It sounds impressive to say we should stay and fight, but how? With what?"

"I know, Melissa. I know. Those tickets for UK, when are we supposed to take the flight?" "I can call and arrange for that whenever you think you are up to it."

"I would like to be able to sell the house first, and I hope to get money out of the bank. I also intend to be paid what I have coming at the office. There is something about being driven from country to country that is bad enough. Being cheated out of property and wages in every one of them is adding insult to injury."

Melissa had expected them to pack a bag or two

and just abandon everything after Tonio's close call at the detention camp. In spite of the danger, she was glad to hear him say he still wasn't willing to pack it all in.

"I agree with you, Tonio, but if at any time we think we are in real danger for our lives again, let's give up and leave."

"Agreed. Now please pull the curtains, I am going to go to sleep."

CHAPTER FOURTEEN

She left the room thinking that every hour that passed made it more likely that their bank account would be frozen. She looked at her bank book and read that there were fifty six thousand shillings in the bank. The sum stopped her for a moment. The same amount that she needed in order to ransom herself from Zanzibar. She knew only too well what that amount of money meant.

She called for her servant, "Amina, I am going down to the bank and I would like you to come with me if you are not afraid, and if your husband says it's all right. I don't think anything will happen to me if I am with an African. I feel sure that there is no danger in it for you, or I wouldn't ask you. But talk to your husband first, we will go if he says it is all right."

The maid hurried off and came back in a moment with a shopping basket. "We will go. He will stay with Bwana and keep doors locked."

Melissa was determined to be with as many people as she could be—even a taxi might be stopped and any Asian pulled out of it. But she didn't think the police or soldiers would take anyone off a bus full of people.

The bank was busier than usual for the time of day. Most of the people in line were Asian. She stood in a long line with Amina standing at her side while the line inched slowly forward. It was evident that people were withdrawing not depositing. The tellers kept looking anxiously behind them at the clock, the people in line were very quiet.

Everyone had his own thoughts and none of them was in any position to help anyone else. It was just too late to do anything but withdraw what they could.

When Melissa got to the window, she asked in a low voice to withdraw all her funds. The teller excused himself and went off to talk to a superior who spread his hands wide, shrugged and laughed quietly. The teller looked back at Melissa and said something further and the other man made some concession, because the teller came back and said, "We cannot let you take it all out now, but we can give you twenty thousand shillings and perhaps later..."

Melissa didn't say anything, so he asked again, "Shall I give you the money?"

"Yes, by all means and thank you very much."

"It is nothing," he said and counted the money out to her as she made the check out in the amount of twenty thousand shillings. She knew and the teller knew that she was taking out all she would be allowed to take and that she was very lucky to have that much.

It made a huge bundle. She watched as he counted it out and then, rather than have it seen by everyone when she turned from the counter, she stuffed it quickly into the large purse she carried with her.

She turned around then and she and Amina walked quickly out of the bank. There was a bus on the corner and they ran to catch it.

"This not our bus, Mem Sahib!" Amina gasped fearfully.

"I know, but it goes to a corner where ours will stop and no one else got on but us at this stop." She was speaking in a very low voice and wasn't sure if Amina understood her, but she seemed to and when Melissa signaled that they should get off, the older woman followed without question. With this round about method it took longer to go home, but they arrived without being followed or stopped.

Tonio was still asleep and Hassani was sleeping just as soundly on the floor beside the bed. She tiptoed out, told Amina where her husband was and that she should go out back to her house and rest since she wouldn't be needed until the next day.

Then she set to work making a light-weight money belt out of cotton material to carry ten thousand shillings. She didn't have a machine and it was rather slow work because she wanted it to be a secure place for the money and yet it mustn't show under her clothes. When it was finished, she put half the money in it and immediately put it right on under her slip. She looked at herself in the mirror from every angle.

Nothing showed. Then she set about making a larger one which Tonio would have to wear to carry the other half. it seemed like a lot, but altogether that twenty thousand shillings would be only about eleven hundred pounds in England or three thousand dollars in Canada. it might be all they could hope to take with them.

She heard Tonio and the servant talking and went in. Hassani was giving Tonio fresh water.

"How are you feeling?"

"Much better. We both had a good rest." Hassani put down his water pitcher, and left. He was glad to have things under some order again, and his own wife safe. "Tonio, while you were sleeping, I went out and got our money out of the bank. That is to say, all they would let us have—twenty thousand shillings. I made us two money belts, half for each. We will need to wear them because I feel sure they will go through our luggage and probably our wallets, too. I doubt we will be stripped, so when you get dressed put this on first." She handed him her clumsy looking homemade money belt.

"I wouldn't have let you go out if I'd known where you were going."

"I know that, but I was certain Amina and I would have a better chance of getting the money out than you would. Men don't take women as seriously as they do other men, but they don't think of us as much of a threat either."

Tonio smiled. "Little do we know, I suppose. Hand me a mirror, will you please? I want to see if I look decent enough to go to work tomorrow."

"You don't plan to work!"

"No, I don't. I do plan to ask for my wages. I have quite a bit of money owed me. I worked for it and I want to try to collect it."

"Tonio, the bank was full of Asians trying to get money out. I noticed most of the shops are already closed, there are great lines of people waiting around the office of the British High Commissioner, too. The planes to England are supposed to be full and some of those people just keep going back and forth between here and London.

England won't accept them because they aren't British subjects or because they don't have visas, The newspapers sound awful. Even allowing for the usual exaggeration, things are very grim."

"Yes, but who knows, maybe I will be able to sell the house to the Libyan embassy. They are great friends of Idi Amin."

"I wish you wouldn't try, Tonio. It is true they are friends, but they will probably simply call up the Government ministry in charge of housing and ask that our house be given to them. We would have put them in a position to get it even quicker than they would have if they bought it."

"You're right. Let's try some charitable organizations. We could offer them the use of this house without charge, let's say for a five year period. That way it would be worth their while to accept and to move in. After five years, we can either give it to them, possibly even rent it to them, come back and live in it, or perhaps by then the government will have taken it over no matter who is living in it."

"Tonio, that's the best idea so far."

They phoned the priest who married them and asked him to come over if he possibly could. In about an hour he was there at the door.

"Come in, Father, we have a strange request to

make of you. We have to abandon our home and everything in it, because our position here has become very dangerous. I don't know what your situation is, perhaps not much better?"

"I'm afraid it isn't. But I plan to stay until they throw me out bodily. My parish is mainly black. They don't object to me and my work is here. I belong to a religious order so I have nothing of material value to lose and no family. How can I be of service to you?"

They explained that they hoped he would know of a religious group who could use their home for the next five years.

"I will try to find one. Normally, there would be several religious orders that would be glad to have it, but some have already been asked to leave, and others aren't allowed to do their usual work. There is a group working on African Dialects and Languages. They plan to put out some scriptural studies in Lugala and Baganda. They are Christian and doing scholarly work. I think they might be happy to accept.

You have a phone here, so I'll call right away." He called and a group from the society came out in less than an hour.

They were grateful for the offer and delighted to accept. They said that if their work were done within five years or if they had to leave, they would try to leave it in the care of some other worthy organization. "We hope that eventually you will get your home back."

"Yes, but if we don't, at least this way it will be used for a good purpose." She couldn't help but think she was glad it wouldn't be sold to friends of ldi Amin.

Melissa showed them around and said that they had family photos and things they wanted to save, like her wedding dress. "If you hear from us, will you kindly send the boxes under the stairs along to us? They are the family things I mentioned and some linens. If you never hear from us, well, just use the things, we truly hope to escape and settle elsewhere, but...'"

"Now, now, don't talk like that." chided Father Ruis. "You are leaving here, but you will be heard from and soon. Have good heart!" But he didn't sound too certain either.

Melissa wondered if she should offer tea or something, but she didn't feel up to doing that. The group thanked them again, told them not to be too concerned because they would take good care of things both inside the house and in the garden.

Melissa asked them to keep Hassani and Amina on and living in the little dwelling behind the main house. They were even glad to have servants already on the property and would pay them the same wages.

When everyone left Tonio said, "'This is our last night here."

"Yes, my love, our last night."

He put his arm around her shoulders and together they saw to the locking of the doors and windows. They left lights on all over the house, and then went into their own bedroom and locked the door.

Sometime during the night Melissa dreamed of an ice cream parlor she liked in Dar. In the morning she was about to tell Tonio about it when he said, "'Remember the ice cream parlor we used to go to in Dar? Chap at work told me that the couple who ran it moved to Australia where he is running the same kind of business and doing well."

"Tonio, what an odd coincidence. I dreamed about that place last night. Perhaps because I have been wanting a good dish of chocolate ice cream."

"Maybe, but do think about Australia. It is warm, we could live near the sea. Shall we see about a visa for Australia?"

"'We probably should. It is best to have a goal, a place where we would really like to live, or, I suppose we could go back to Tanzania at least for awhile."

"Yes. I know we could, but it might be the same thing all over again, or at least the fear of it. Our children would be second class citizens."

Melissa felt a pang of sadness hearing "*our children*" because no little ones seemed to want to make an appearance.

CHAPTER FIFTEEN

"**W**ell, if you are ready, let's take the bus. I'll show you where to get off for the Australian High Commission and I'll join you there as soon as I get my wages.'"

"As soon as you don't get them, more likely!"

"The servants!" Tonio exclaimed. "'We must pay them what we owe them plus an extra five hundred shillings. In Tanzania one has to pay an extra month wages at termination and I think that is a very good and reasonable thing. And of course, be sure to tell them that their home is still here and they will have the same wages."

Melissa hurried out to talk to Amina and Hassani. They were sad to see Tonio and Melissa go, but pleased that they would not have to look for new lodgings or a new place to work.

"We will be back later to get our bags and would appreciate one more meal in this house. You just fix us whatever you can, and what is left is for you. Take any remaining supplies." Melissa tried to smile but just couldn't. It didn't help her that Amina kept swallowing so she wouldn't cry.

Tonio and Melissa set out with the usual flow of traffic going to work. He showed her the best place to get off for the Australian High Commission and he continued on to his office.

There was a new guard on duty at the door who didn't recognize him. The guard called inside to have a clerk come out.

"Yes, that's a member of the staff, let him in."

"Why all the care at the door?" Tonio asked as the two of them walked down the hallway together.

"We have been having threats against Asians and after we learned what happened to you, we are extra careful."

"Is the paymaster in?"

"Yes, in his office."

Tonio walked over to that office and applied for the wages he had coming.

The paymaster looked uneasy, "Do you not intend to return to your post?"

"No, I will not be back."

"Really, you are giving too much importance to a highly unusual occurrence. One policeman mistakes you for someone else and has you beaten. This is not the normal thing."

"No indeed. Nor is the camp I was in, and would still be in, if we hadn't shown tickets to UK and not argued with the guard who stole our car."

The paymaster had no answer to this but seemed disgusted with him. He went through the records and proceeded to pay out what was owed for that month, but not the money that had been withheld in the first month of work.

Tonio explained what was lacking.

The man returned to his ledgers and then, very unwillingly, paid out the remaining sum.

Tonio was about to thank him, and then, realizing that the man had intended to cheat him and probably would have taken the extra sum for himself saying that Tonio had collected it, he merely looked hard at the man and strode off to his old office.

In the hall he passed several people he knew. Most were very concerned about him and glad to see him recovered from the beating, and they were angry about it. The people he considered his friends did not suggest that he stay. They seemed to recognize the danger he was in. But it was also evident that there were several others who really enjoyed his predicament.

Two secretaries looked at each other and giggled when they saw him. "They would have loved to watch the beating," he thought bitterly. One of the accountants got up and slammed the door hard as Tonio passed by. Tonio knew why, too. The man had been cheating the government for a long time, now he could do it without Tonio's complaints. He knows I feel contempt for his dishonesty, so he hates me. Very simple.

To Tonio's surprise, the African chief Auditor was in Tonio's office when he walked in.

"You are back! Good."

"Not really. Just came to collect my wages and to show you where I am with my cases so you can assign them to other men." Tonio explained several cases, put notations on some and said, "Well, that about does it. I'll be off now." He wasn't sure how the African felt about him, and it was not a good idea to ask.

The black man stood half a head taller than Tonio

and weighed at least three stone more. He shyly extended his hand for Tonio to shake as though he expected him to refuse. Tonio was glad to take his hand and surprised when the other man patted his shoulder and said, "Pole sana, all so useless, so sad." The look of sorrow was obvious.

"Tell your wife that my family and I extend our best wishes to you both. All of us who were at your wedding were talking about your problem and we are just sickened by it. That is why we put another guard at the door. By the way, our little boy still talks about your wedding. The first he ever attended."

"Oh yes, he was the little fellow who got into the mint candies and got sick at the reception?" Both men laughed and the tension was gone. Tonio wished he had some memento to give him. Then he remembered, "Here, this is for the little rascal!" and he brought from his desk a pack of ballpoint pens, colored pencils and a stapler he'd bought to replace the pins that were always used.

The big man laughed like a child, and said, "Oh, my little boy will be delighted!" The two of them walked down the hall and were joined by several others, all of those who had been at his wedding, he noted.

They accompanied him to the door of the building, offered many good wishes and all shook his hand warmly. He realized there were tears in his eyes as he turned and walked toward the bus stop.

There was only a short line at the Australian High Commission by the time Tonio joined Melissa, who was by then the third in line. All Asians but one, and he appeared to be English. They talked to a First Secretary who asked them what they planned to do for a living.

"I am an accountant, familiar with the English system. I have taken some of my Charter Exams and will finish within a year or so, I hope."

"Good. Do you have sufficient funds?"

"We have twenty thousand shillings which is all we were allowed to take out and two tickets to England which we will turn in for cash. We have a home here and some property in Kenya. We hope to be able to take money from Kenya with us."

"No other dependents?"

"None," Melissa answered weakly.

"Here, this will enable you to enter as immigrants. The gentleman at the desk there has other materials for you. You will also have to see to vaccinations and so on." He smiled pleasantly at them and waved the next person forward.

"I feel so insignificant. Like a chair that gets moved from one place to another," Melissa complained.

"Well, there is this—it certainly must be a good remedy for pride! It will always be impossible for us to think that there is any place on earth that would be hard pressed to do without us."

"Yes indeed. By the way, did you get your pay?"

"I did. All of it. And most of the staff were very good to me, too. Walked me down to the door and wished us both well."

"When you mentioned twenty thousand shillings, I rather supposed they had not paid you."

"I simply forgot it. I am so conscious of the ten thousand shillings around my middle that I forget what I have in my wallet," he said with a laugh.

"Let's go home now and have lunch and then see about a flight to Nairobi. We can stay there long enough to see Mr. Montero and get what money we can and find a ship that sails for Australia from Mombasa."

"A ship?" he asked rather incredulously.

"Yes. I would rather land in true immigrant fashion, by ship, would you?"

"Hadn't thought about it. Just assumed we would go by air. Did you give any thought to where we should live there? It is a big place you know."

"Yes, I think we should go to Adelaide. It is on the sea and we like the sea. Another reason for going by ship."

Tonio shrugged, gave her hand a squeeze and said, "Why not?"

When they arrived home, they found a good lunch of cold meat salad and fresh fruit ready for them. They ate it slowly, called a taxi, put two bags for each of them into the taxi and with a last goodbye to the servants they left their home. There was a flight at three to Nairobi and a huge crowd of Asians already at the airport, most waiting for flights to UK.

A surly bank of black soldiers with rifles slung over their shoulders were jostling the Asians and taking gold bangles from the arms of the women.

One soldier had several rings on his little finger. Like many others, he had been drinking and Melissa felt sure that he would have lost most of the rings by evening. It was both disgusting and frightening.

Their flight to Nairobi was called and with a sense of relief they walked through the gate to board it. It was then that the soldier with all the rings and one other one asked to see their identification. They pushed Tonio and Melissa to the side and winked at one another drunkenly. Tonio held her arm firmly and tried to brush past the soldiers, but they showed that their rifles were loaded and ready to fire when one of them released the safety with an ominous click.

A stewardess stood at the doorway of the plane and called a steward to come quickly. He did, but there was nothing he could do either, except watch.

The two soldiers went through Tonio's wallet, took out the money he had been paid that morning and stuffed it into their own pockets.

Melissa had given up the tickets at the gate and had boarding passes in her hand.

She could see that Tonio was about to strike one of the men, which probably would lead to his being shot. She was gripped by fear and no one stopped to help them.

What could anyone do against drunken, heavily armed men? No one wanted to be shot, nor to lose a husband wife or child. All of them had gone through so much, now to miss their chance to escape seemed foolish since they couldn't win. Every window of the plane on the side facing them was full of people watching fearfully.

Then along came their old servant, Hassani. He was staggering toward them and screaming that

Tonio and Melissa were capitalist monsters, exploiters of the people.

He could hardly pronounce the words, but his whole manner was loud and offensive.

Tonio looked stunned and Melissa felt sick and so hurt and bewildered she couldn't take her eyes off the old man.

The soldiers, thinking they had taken all there was to take, let Hassani approach them. They laughed at the drunken old man and said, "Too late, too late!"

"No, not too late to spit in face of Asian dogs." He got up close to Melissa, grabbed her hand angrily and pressed something inside it. At the same time he rudely pushed his other hand into Tonio's coat pocket.

They whispered *"Thank you"* and walked up the stairway of the plane.

"Why didn't you push that drunken old fool away?" the steward asked indignantly.

Tonio answered softly, "That drunken old fool is a devout Muslim who never touches alcohol. He brought us some valuables we had forgotten to take. He took the only way he had to return them to us. A brave old man."

Melissa was looking at the palm of her hand and trying not to cry. Hassani had brought her aunt's rings to her. He couldn't give them the jewel box, so he had chosen the things of greatest value and carried them in his hands. In Tonio's pocket was a wrist-watch and a diamond ring.

"I feel so sorry for Hassani, he must have been embarrassed. A terrible thing for a him to pretend to be a drunken, racist old fool." Melissa sighed deeply.

Tonio started to chuckle. Finally he was actually laughing aloud. "He even had us fooled for a moment. That old man would have made a great actor. I don't feel sorry for him at all. He will go home and tell this story to his wife and to his children when they come to visit and everyone will laugh and have fun over it. He was probably afraid when he did it, but believe me, he is laughing now."

"I suppose you are right."

Melissa felt better then and put on the rings and felt quite content in spite of it all.

CHAPTER SIXTEEN

Nairobi was its usual bustling self, and as usual Melissa was cold. "I'll phone Mr. Montero as soon as we get to the hotel and he can advise us on what to do next," she said as she shivered in the cool weather.

"Good. I'll get newspapers and find out when there is a sailing from Mombasa for Australia."

Neither of them mentioned Uganda, nor their home there. By a sort of common agreement that was unspoken, neither of them talked about anything but the present and ideas for the future. Sometimes Melissa had a dry taste in her mouth and bitter feelings, the same as she had in Zanzibar, but she knew she had to ignore them.

She was glad they had decided on the sea voyage. They needed some time to quietly adjust. There had been too many violent changes in too short a time.

Montero was delighted to hear her voice and know that she and Tonio were safe in Nairobi. "The BOAC Manager called me when you were detained, rather, when Tonio was, amounts to the same thing."

"Can you come over to the New Stanley Coffee Shop and join us for a little while?"

"I certainly can. Be right with you."

Melissa and Tonio were hardly seated when Montero arrived, smiling broadly at seeing them well.

Tonio thanked him for all he'd done for Melissa and asked him what chance he thought there was of getting her money out of Kenya.

"I think it is fairly good. She has more money there than they will let you take out at one time. However, I have not presented my bill. It may well be extremely high."

Both of them knew that his bill would be reasonable and that he would simply return the extra money to them so that they could start over. "That is very good of you!" Melissa exclaimed.

"Not at all, it is your money, you know. But the rent from the government that goes into a separate rental account is something else. I suggest you leave it there for the time being You can take it out, bit by bit."

"Mr. Montero, we plan to emigrate to Australia." Melissa said.

"Australia!" Montero exclaimed and added, "Well yes, I can understand that. I hope it works out well for you, better than Uganda did."

Neither of them spoke for a moment and then Tonio said truthfully, "Uganda was good to us in many ways. We were very happy there and we met some people we will never forget, wonderful, kind people. Well, yes, and some very bad people too." He shook his head slowly as if in disbelief and Melissa hurriedly asked him if he wouldn't like to have something to eat along with his tea.

A ship was leaving in two days for Australia from Mombasa and the steamship line in Nairobi made passage arrangements for them. They went to a doctor and had the necessary inoculations. This made them feel queasy in the stomach and very sore in the arm so they did little but write short notes to friends in Zanzibar and Tanzania telling them that they were on their way to Adelaide and would write again when they had an address.

"The lines that tie us to Zanzibar and Tanzania, to Africa itself, seem to be getting cut." Tonio commented.

"I hope not, I hope I will always be able to have a letter now and then from Zanzibar and from friends in East Africa." There was a catch in her voice.

Tonio said gently, "Yes, things are not usually this bad here. No need for us to suppose that they will stay this way. Who knows, perhaps we were always meant to be Australians?"

Mr. Montero drove them to the airport for the short flight to Mombasa, a taxi took them to the dock and suddenly, there it was—a beautiful ocean liner ready to be boarded by passengers going south.

"Look to your right Over in Dhow Harbor—what do you think?" Melissa asked trying not to sound too excited.

"I think that is Saidi's dhow. Let's put our stuff on board the liner and go visiting. We have time!" They locked their things in their stateroom and told the attendant that they would be back in good time. They ran down the beach laughing and shouting, more and more sure that it was Saidi the closer they got.

"Halloooo, Saidi!" Tonio bellowed and down on the beach, not far from his vessel, an Arab stood up and shaded his eyes as he looked toward them. He dropped his little coffee cup and ran with long strides on the firm sand.

"Melissa, Tonio—what are you doing here?"

"We are on our way to Australia." she pointed to the liner. They were too excited to sit down and talk so they walked up and down the beach telling each other what had happened since Melissa was lowered into the water near Dar es Salaam.

"I have seen your relatives in Zanzibar several times. I call on them when I am in Zanzibar Town and they have told me about the trouble in Nairobi and your narrow escapes. I knew that you and Tonio were married, too. I have other news for you.

Your cousins have decided to emigrate. You will never guess where they are going."

The Arabs weather beaten face glowed with his news.

Because of his smile, Melissa guessed Australia and he said, "Yes, but I have forgotten the city. It is the name of a woman."

"Adelaide?" Melissa asked, her heart pounding with hope.

"Yes. That is it."

Then Saidi told them of his travels and that he thought he might settle down as a resident of Abu Dhabi on the gulf of Arabia. "There is much money there, oil money. Other Arabs are welcome, and it is not a bad idea to be welcome. I could find that a nice change." He grinned and his big strong teeth glistened in his sun-darkened face.

"You won't settle down on land, will you?" asked Melissa.

"I don't suppose I will, but if there is oil money, there will be people wanting to spend it and I will help them by providing the goods to buy. I may make enough to buy a better vessel. I think dhows are finally going out of date. Still, there is nothing like the Indian Ocean at night, and sleeping on a dhow that creaks and groans and brings pleasant rest."

"Will we see you again?" Melissa asked hopefully.

"Inshallah – Allah knows. Maybe not here. Maybe in Australia."

He embraced them both and then Tonio and Melissa ran back to their ship, greatly encouraged by seeing the tough Arab sailor who questioned nothing, but put his trust in God.

"Imagine, Tonio, Rita and her family are going to be in Adelaide too! We won't be alone after all."

"Oh, we wouldn't be all alone, they tell me Adelaide is a large city."

She threw a pillow at him and then lay down intending to get a good rest.

The ship pulled away from the shore, the beach disappeared and then the palm trees. Finally nothing could be seen of the city of Mombasa.

Tonio was standing looking out the porthole and musing aloud, "I can't see Fort Jesus anymore. How little good fortresses seem to do. The Portuguese built Fort Jesus to keep the Arabs and Zulus out, yet Mombasa is full of Arabs and blacks of many tribes and you hardly ever see a Portuguese."

"I don't think I have ever seen one," allowed Melissa, she was trying to get comfortable enough to fall asleep.

"Someone in our families must have, since we all have Portuguese names."

Melissa hadn't expected to be so seasick, so she was surprised when she couldn't keep her meals down, she felt faint, couldn't sleep and had fierce headaches.

Finally, Tonio asked the ship's doctor to look in on her. While the doctor examined her, Tonio walked round the deck hoping it wouldn't be anything serious. They had come so far and struggled against so much injustice, now when they were about to land, Melissa was really sick. When he saw the doctor leave, he hurried back into the cabin. Forcing himself to keep his voice from trembling, he asked what the doctor said. Melissa opened her arms wide to him and said softly, "He said that you are going to be the father of an Australian!"